# CHOSEN BY THE MAGES

A SEASONAL SPICE COLLECTION

BOUND BY THE MAGES

THE WITCH'S TANGLE

L.A. MONTEIRO

CHAOS ELF PUBLISHING

# CONTENT NOTES

This book contains MFM open-door sex scenes, and some light BDSM (bondage, domination, sadism and masochism).
If you're not sure what that means you're probably reading the wrong book.

This collection includes the second and third books in the Seasonal Spice series, and features characters from 50 Shades of Orc, but can be read as an entry point into the series.

# CONTENTS

Bound by the Mages

## The Witch's Tangle

# BOUND BY THE MAGES

L.A. MONTEIRO

CHAOS ELF PUBLISHING

# Chapter One

## CASSIA

Cassia frowns in concentration at the cauldron on her stove. Bright pink liquid bubbles inside it. *So far so good.* Symphonic metal screams from the speaker beside her, but she barely hears it.

Steel bowls lie scattered around her on a vintage-look kitchen counter, and she holds a vial of red flower petals in her hand.

She tips the vial above the cauldron and taps it gently with her finger. Petals float down towards the surface. *One... Two...*

The pounding at the door shakes the room. The bowls around her clank together. Her hand shakes, and two more petals fall into the cauldron. The bubbling pink liquid turns brown.

*Shit.*

She slams the vial down and flicks off the speaker next to her. It's wired through the house, not just this room. Silence falls abruptly. She storms down the corridor towards the door, past half-painted walls and a ladder she keeps meaning to move. The floorboards are streaked with scratches.

The glass panel strips on the front door are rattling from the knocking. It's an old house, and the knocking could crack the glass. *What kind of arrogant asshole...*

She throws the door open, hands on hips, ready to confront whoever interrupted her spell.

Her heart leaps in her chest.

It's one of the mage brothers who moved next door. Not the sexy one with the motorbike and the mess of dark hair. The other one, who looks as stiff as a lawyer representing a high class client in court.

He's still pretty, she has to admit. His hair is artfully arranged atop his head in a modern cut, short on the sides and back. Coiffed designer stubble offsets his square jaw. He's wearing a suit with an old-fashioned blue cravat, even though he can't be older than she is - around 30 to her 25. The cravat is almost a bow - like a gift.

*Special delivery. And way hotter than my infuriating ex Darren.*

The thought is an unwelcome intrusion. She's not thinking about Darren and his effortless charm and pretty face. If she thinks about him, then she thinks about what he did to her. From there, her thoughts go to the mess in the kitchen and what it means for her business and her life. Better to focus on the pretty boy in front of her, who ruined her potion.

"What do you want?" she snaps.

"For a start, you could turn the music down," he says, blue eyes icy under furrowed brows. There's an arrogant glint in his eye. Of course, there is - he's a mage. They think they're the only magic users who matter.

"It's 6pm," she points out.

He arches a single eyebrow. "So?"

"So, it's not a late hour. No other neighbors have complained." She doesn't add that a 'don't notice me' spell doubles as a noise blocker to non-magic users. Her only other magically inclined neighbor, Mrs Maisley, is a doddery old witch with poor hearing.

He's unmoved. "I'm complaining now."

"If you don't like the noise, maybe you shouldn't have moved in."

He stares her down. Her eyes meet his with equal challenge. She hates entitled men most of all. His beauty makes him even more irritating.

Although his gaze doesn't waver, eventually he clears his throat and speaks in a clipped tone. "My name is Lincoln West, and I recently moved in next door with my brother, Bradley. Although we were aware there were witches in the area, we didn't think it would be an issue to have neighbors who want to play with magic. We're respectful people. I expect the same courtesy."

His eyes drift past her. The door to the front bedroom is ajar. It's layered in drop cloths, paint cans and other signs of an abandoned renovation. She bristles, feeling his judgment from his shiny shoes to his coiffed hair.

It doesn't help that her hair's a rat's nest, kept in place in a loose bun atop her head. She's wearing her oldest black cotton dress and an apron splattered in old potions. And she barely slept last night trying to get this spell right. She looks awful. She feels awful. And his nose is pointed up like she's something scraped off his shoe.

She folds her arms.

"Well, Mr West, my name is Cassia Theseira, and I think it's just like a mage to expect the world to bend to them. Just because mages specialize in one kind of magic and don't use spells doesn't make you better than witches. And I was in Oakford first, Lincoln, so don't expect me to change my lifestyle because I have new neighbors. If you don't like it, you can call the police and make a noise complaint. Good luck with that." She slams the door in his face.

_____ ◊ _____

Back in the kitchen, hands on hips, she scowls at the cauldron. A bubble rises and bursts on the brown surface. Gross. She reaches into the front pocket of her apron and pulls out a vial labeled "Love Potion." A thick pink liquid sparkles inside it. It's a far cry from the mess in the cauldron.

Damn him! The potion is an extremely finicky spell. It has to be made at a precise and consistent temperature, and the key ingredient - fresh red hemlock flowers - is almost impossible to get.

Dread sinks her stomach. Without the potion, there's no money. Without money there's no mortgage payments, and no beautiful house or independent life. She's sunk everything she has into her gift business, and this pink goo is at the root of it all. She's perfected the recipe - refined it even from her mother's spell, and a couple of drops goes into everything she sells. It's not enough to really affect people, but enough to make them feel connected to their loved ones, and enough to make her business profitable.

She had it all worked out before Darren Brently came back into her life, with a sob story about leaving the coven, just like her. Beautiful Darren Brently, who she'd always had a crush on. Treacherous Darren Brently who ruined her.

She shakes her head against the rising frustration at past mistakes and pulls her phone out of her apron pocket. She hits contacts. There are only five saved - all clients. And only one worth asking for help. She dials, turning away from the cauldron and walking into the hall.

"Hey you," a woman's voice answers, low and suggestive, hip hop blaring in the background.

"Olivia! Hi! I was hoping you could help. I'm out of red hemlock flowers and I'm having issues with suppliers. Could you possibly grab me some from your local witch shop? I'd pay, of course, and throw in a discount on your next buy. I'm stuck at home right now, up to my eyeballs in packing orders, or I'd go myself." Cassia stands still in the hallway, holding her breath. She hopes Olivia buys the flimsy reason she can't leave the house.

Olivia is a new client, and unaffiliated with Cassia's old coven. She buys sleeping potions and a quick-healing salve for abrasions and skin irritations. They met by accident at a bulk-buy herbal store and Olivia asked her for advice. Or rather, Olivia tried to pick Cassia up, Cassia politely declined, and Olivia became a client. A human client. Cassia's not even sure how much Olivia believes in magic.

As far as the human world is concerned, magic doesn't exist. This is despite the fact a couple hundred orcs arrived through a portal a few years ago and remain stranded on earth. Somehow, humans have compartmentalized the existence of orcs and portals as freak science. They remain oblivious to the witches and mages who live among them.

Fortunately, this means humans are totally oblivious to witch politics, which Cassia's in up to her eyeballs. Right now, Olivia's the closest thing to a friend Cassia has, which is a sad thought Cassia can deal with once she's out of this mess.

"I'll take that discount and order a double - it's working great and I'm sure I'll need more. I feel bad buying wholesale directly from you though - never thought of selling direct to the public online yourself?" asks Olivia.

"Oh no, um, I'm no good at that stuff. I'm happy as I am, to be honest, just needing those extra supplies," Cassia says quickly, continuing her walk into the front room of her house.

Growing up in a sheltered witch's coven hadn't exactly made her tech savvy. Witches had an understandable but outdated fear of anything that could track them. Leaving the coven had been a sharp learning curve. She could get her head around selling to shopfront owners. Running a website, not so much. And so far, she hasn't needed to sell any other way.

"Ah well, gorgeous, it's always nice to hear from you. How are you going? That sexy warlock still keeping you happy?"

"Oh... good, yeah. He's good. And you?" Her free hand anxiously rubs her forehead. Her front room is empty of furniture, and a stack of painting supplies are stashed in the corner. The rest of the floor is covered in crates of bright pink packages. Massage oil, moisturizer, lip balms, perfumes and candles.

This is her entire next shipment - everything left after Darren took off two months ago with her life savings and her entire stock. Thank god she doesn't have any friends, or she'd be seriously embarrassed right now.

"Cass, you don't sound great. What's really going on?" Cassia's free fist clenches involuntarily at Olivia's words. Olivia is sharp - it's something Cassia liked about her instantly when they met. Right now, it's a pain in the ass.

"Nothing! Just... stressed about shipments is all, but like I said, I really can't get out. I don't suppose you could get the hemlock soon?"

"Of course! When do you need it by?

Yesterday? she thinks, but out loud says, "The sooner the better - would tomorrow be too crazy?"

"How about tonight? I'm in your area anyway, and we can catch up."

Cassia's fist unclenches. "Thank you so much." She hangs up the phone and sighs.

Maybe everything will be alright after all. She'll avoid her witch contacts for a while, keep trading with ordinary human suppliers, and pick up the pieces. She's always been an optimist.

She could get past the fact her ex was working on behalf of her old coven to sabotage her business. Maybe she should take it as a positive sign - she was doing so well, they saw her as a threat to their own ventures. But she needs to keep her head above water while she figures out how to stay afloat without treading on the coven's toes. And make sure the protection wards on her house are strong enough to keep Darren away in case he decides to pay another visit.

Tomorrow she'll finish the potion, but tonight, she's stuck in her house. Her mind drifts to the noise complaint earlier. Lincoln was clearly an ass, which makes her wonder about the brother who didn't visit. Definitely a "Brad" rather than "Bradley". He wears a leather jacket and white t-shirts that mold nicely to his shoulders.

She walks around the bottom floor, checking her wards at each window and door. They're all in place, but they'll need replacing soon, by someone better at wards than she is. She hasn't trusted any local witches after the Darren incident, and she can't afford to hire in an out of towner. At least right now there's not much left for him to steal.

Walking up the stairs, the skin on her arms goosebumps as the sun sets. Upgrading the heating in the living areas is one of many things on her renovation list. Hopefully, Olivia will come through with what she needs tomorrow. But right now, she can't do any more, and she's glad to call it a day. It's about this time Brad gets home next door and takes a shower. The view into his bathroom is just the night cap she needs.

# CHAPTER TWO

# LINCOLN

Lincoln's irritation drops a notch when he steps through his front door. The house makes him proud. The original dark wooden floorboards shine with health, and the hallway is newly painted a crisp white. They've only been here a week, but he's already got it set up exactly as he wants it.

Their home is a vintage Californian bungalow like Cassia's, but theirs is in much better shape. It's a combination of vintage charm and modern conveniences. And it's all theirs - the first thing they've owned independent of the mage community they grew up in.

Brad is in the kitchen, facing the sink and looking at the neat line of herbs in white pots in front of the picture window. He still has his leather jacket and motorcycle boots on. The air smells faintly of motor oil and blood.

Then he turns around. He has a glass full of water in one hand and a couple of pills in the other. A bruise is rising on his right cheek, a cut on his lip. Specks of blood dot his shirt. The violence on his face contrasts sharply with the cream cupboards and oiled wooden benches around him. He takes the pills and washes them down.

His eyes are tired, but he grins, then winces as the cut on his lip bleeds. With his smooth jaw, paler features and scruffy hair, Brad has boyish good looks that make people ask whether they're brothers by blood. They're not, but as far as Lincoln's concerned, that's nobody else's business.

"Making friends with the locals?" Lincoln asks.

"I'm real friendly. How did your thing go?"

"I didn't have a chance to ask her," Lincoln evades, scowling.

"Wasn't that the whole reason you went over there?"

"Her music was so loud I couldn't hear myself think. And then she answered the door, and she was so rude..."

Brad rolls his eyes. "Were you a dick about it?"

"She was rude to me. I asked her to turn her music down."

"So you were a dick about it," Brad confirms.

Lincoln frowns but otherwise ignores him. "She probably doesn't have the skills we need, anyway. And Vera can give us the connections to find someone else."

Brad scowls. His lip is almost healed. "I trust Vera as much as I can throw her. And isn't that why you moved us here? Because of the witches?"

"It was one option," Lincoln says icily. He knows he messed up, but he won't stand here and let his little brother lecture him. "I won't tolerate rudeness from the witch. We've had enough of that to last a lifetime. We don't take shit from people. That was our mother's downfall - it won't be ours."

"This isn't Healesville, Lincoln," Brad says. "The witch doesn't even know who we are. Stop being a dick and offer her money. Girls like shiny things, remember?" He drinks the rest of the water.

Lincoln watches him. The bruise on Brad's face is already gone. The healing pills he just downed are amazing, but they no longer have access to more. An arrangement with a witch will have more than one use.

"Are you out tonight?" Lincoln asks lightly, trying not to let his tension show. Brad was always bitter and angry. It wasn't easy on them growing up bastard half-bloods in a mage community. But since their mother died six months ago, he's been outright reckless.

Brad shakes his head. "Irene doesn't like it when we both go out." He leaves it at that, but Lincoln knows he's worried. Irene hasn't been the same since they left

Healesville. Her leaves have been droopy and drier than normal.

She might just be a plant, but she has enough magic in her to have real feelings. Last time she got upset she ripped a hole in their bathroom wall in pique, and kidnapped the neighbour's dog, keeping it in a cage of vines until Lincoln made her let it go.

"She's just sulking. You shouldn't spoil her. Remember when she had a tantrum when mum tried to buy us a cat? If you give in, she'll never learn. Promise me you won't go out there tonight."

"She's allowed a little time to settle in," Brad says in defense.

"If you cave to her, she'll regress and we'll have to retrain her. Promise me."

Brad glares at Lincoln. Lincoln holds firm. Eventually, Brad's eyes slide off to the side. "Fine," he mutters.

Lincoln turns to leave the kitchen. "I'm heading to my office."

"I don't know why you bother. You can't even read that thing," Brad calls out behind him.

Lincoln sighs when he sits down in the leather office chair behind his heavy wooden desk. Matching bookshelves line the wall behind him. It's the office of his dreams, complete with a single red couch in the corner for reading. The only thing on the desk is a big, leather-bound book with yellowing pages.

Lincoln turns a page, and fingers a ripped edge where more pages have been torn out. His mother's grimoire. Before their adopted mother died this year, they didn't know this book existed. She'd turned her back on her witch heritage to find a new life. He has no idea why - magic users stick to their own. She was never truly accepted in Healesville. But she made things better for him and his brother.

The boys had both been the result of mage dalliances with normal people - normies. They had enough magic to keep close, but were still too shameful to claim. They were considered weak for their half blood, and had to prove otherwise with their fists.

Their mother didn't talk about her past, but now she's gone and they have nothing left but memories. Now it's important to know more about her and where she came from. Maybe they could understand more about the woman who adopted them and gave them a home.

The problem is, only a witch can read a grimoire, and most witches live in covens, like most mages live in mage communities. The relationship between the two groups isn't friendly. It's hard to find information on people who live outside the community, but Lincoln moved to Oakford because he could feel the magic in the air. Nothing concrete, just a faint whiff of ozone that said someone was using magic.

The girl next door is definitely a witch. And the old woman on the other side of her is too. He tried to talk to the old woman, but she refused to open the door. He isn't sure if she's hard of hearing or just didn't want to see him.

He shouldn't have snapped at the witch next door. But he was used to fighting his ground. In Healesville, he had to be the hardest fighter, the one who punched first and hardest. That ensured early he never got into fights again, and neither did Brad until he got old enough to start them himself.

In business too, Lincoln had to be the most ruthless. He took over the family business as soon as he was old enough, and pushed his mother to expand, with the ultimate aim of leaving their small community for good. They had the money to do it years ago, but she would never leave, and never tell them why. Now they're left with the question of why she stayed. It seemed like she was running from something, but what? All they had left of her was the grimoire - the book that contained all her secrets. A book he couldn't even read.

He shakes his head, sighing at his musings. When dealing with the witch, maybe he should have been less aggressive.

But she'd surprised him - her arrogance. And he was affected by her pretty face. No, not pretty – she was beautiful. Paired with the way she sneered at him, he'd instinctively lashed out, tried to prove that he didn't care what she thought. If she wanted to reject him, like the entire mage community, then screw her - they would find another way.

# CHAPTER THREE

# CASSIA

C assia stops at the doorway to her bedroom. It always calms her, being in here. This is the only room in the house that's completely finished. The wooden floorboards shine with health, and there's not a speck of dust in the room.

The dark wood moldings and furniture offset nicely with the cream walls she painted herself. The queen-sized wooden bed and ornate dressing table in the corner are worth the exorbitant price she paid. Hell, since she's left the coven, she's even made her bed every day, although no sense of pride will make her clean up the makeup tools all over her dressing table.

Through the bedroom is her tiny ensuite, its cream tiles decorated with tiny pink roses. Many of the tiles are cracked, but she's holding out renovating here until she can afford to replicate the original tiles.

She catches sight of herself in the bathroom mirror. Dark circles sit vividly on her pale skin. She's been overdoing it - stressed about money, struggling with loneliness. It's hard being without a coven, but she doesn't regret the decision to leave.

She'd been independent for almost two years when Darren came knocking on her door, claiming he'd left the coven, too.

The frustrating part of it is that she knows he didn't think of it as stealing, when he took everything she had. What's hers was the coven's, in his eyes. All she needs to do is go back for it - and give all the proceeds of her business to them. Hard pass.

She unties her apron, carefully removing the bottle of potion and setting it down on the vanity next to the sink. It's her sample, and the last vial left Darren didn't take. She hasn't let it out of her sight since he left, even with her protection wards in place. She knows she can make more eventually, and this isn't enough to fulfill her current orders, but somehow having it with her makes her feel safer. Like it's a sign the coven, and Darren, couldn't destroy her business or her hope completely.

She pulls a small pipe, a baggie of witch weed and a lighter from under the sink and puts it next to the vial.

She hoists herself onto the tiny vanity and opens the window. She leaves enough of a gap to stay hidden, but can see down into the bathroom window on the ground floor of the West brothers' house.

Sure enough, the window is wide open, with a clear view straight into the shower. They haven't put up a shower curtain yet. Over the past few nights, while she's enjoying her evening smoke, she's had a good show from the sexy one, not the one with the stick up his ass she met this evening.

She packs her pipe steadily, trying not to get her hopes up. He might have had a shower every night at the same time for the past few days, but that doesn't mean his routine is regular. She'll have a smoke, unwind, and enjoy an early night.

She lights the tangle of herbs and takes a deep inhale, turning around to blow the smoke out the window. Through the window below, the bathroom light is on. She grins to herself as her head spins from the smoke. Then impulsively, she puts the pipe down and shuffles her ass to peel off her panties, throwing them into a waiting hamper with a giggle.

She'll have a shower after this anyway, and it's much easier to masturbate without them on.

She feels only the slightest hint of guilt when the man - Brad, his brother had called him? - steps into the bathroom. How could she not look at him? He's perfection.

His black hair flops into his eyes and she imagines what it would feel like to run her fingers through it. His clean-shaven square jaw offsets pouting lips. He looks insolent, too young for her, and there are specks of blood on his collar. More than once he's come into this bathroom with blood on his clothes. The first time he also had a fat lip. So probably not a serial killer - just a fighter.

He's bad news. Just her type - or the type in her hottest fantasies, anyway.

She never could keep a lid on her libido. She had an active, almost reckless, sex life in the coven, and never wanted for partners. It was considered healthy in young witches to own their own pleasure, and sex was well known as a channel for enhancing magic. But as she got older couples and trios started forming - the normal family units among witches - and she realized none of her lovers considered her a good match.

She was an orphan - protected by the coven but pitied. Magic knowledge was passed down through families in grimoires, and her family and grimoire were both gone.

Witches with long lines had the most powerful families, and they often sought marriage between them.

By the time she left the coven she realized she was using sex as an escape and comfort. It wasn't giving her what she needed. She wanted more.

Darren came from a powerful family. When he turned up on her doorstep, she waited weeks before giving in to her libido, until she was sure there was something between them. And he still betrayed her. Now she knows she's better off alone. If only her body would listen. Fortunately, the boy next door is safely a whole house away. Watching him is uncomplicated fun, and takes the edge off.

From the safety of her own bathroom, she can indulge in all her fantasies of him. Even the things she never trusted any of her lovers enough to do.

He peels off the white t-shirt and her thoughts short-circuit. Muscles stand out on broad shoulders, and tribal tattoos wind around his right shoulder and chest. Her fingers would be put to good use running down the ridges of the abs on his slender framed waist. Instead, they drift down to the softness between her legs.

He steps out of his jeans, and her eyes fixate on his cock. Wetness soaks her fingers, her core tingling with anticipation. The first time she saw him with his pants off, she almost fell out the window. She stops touching herself and takes another puff of smoke, letting a mild haze settle in her mind. No need to rush. He turns on the water. The show's just getting started.

She put the pipe and lighter down blindly, not wanting to turn away from the sight of him. Her fingers graze the potion vial. She braces herself against the vanity and shuffles a bit before leaning out further to get a better view. She has an almost complete view of their back garden, closer to her side of the fence.

A large, healthy fig tree dominates the garden, but along the fence closest to her, she can see sprigs of red flowers. Something about them nags at her attention through the haze in her mind.

The sight of Brad in the shower draws her eyes again, and the thought drops away.

The water runs liberally along the curves of his body and he closes his eyes as he runs his hands through his hair. He's perfectly silhouetted.

She teases her clitoris gently with the tips of her fingers, knowing it won't take long tonight. Fortunately he enjoys a long shower, almost as if he knows he's putting on a show. He reaches for his own cock, stroking it in strong and confident movements, and she imagines kneeling before him and suckling on the tip while he stares down at her.

Maybe he's holding her hair in one fist, hovering on the edge of pain. Maybe her hands are tied behind her back.

An invisible thread runs from the scene before her and the tingling between her legs. She imagines it's his hand, touching her, teasing her, and she presses herself harder, matching speed with Brad's long strokes.

Watching him come into his hand is enough to tip her over the edge in her own release. All her muscles clench, the day dropping away in the flood of ecstasy.

In the aftermath, tension drops from her shoulders and she smiles to herself.

Her gaze drifts from Brad, and the nagging thought she's been successfully ignoring comes back. She looks back at the red flowers. There's something about them....

A jolt of urgency cuts through the haze of lust and smoke. The flowers are red hemlock.

Were the flowers always there, and she never noticed, or were they new? Red hemlock takes months to grow - they must have always been there.

She leans out further to get a better look - her entire body is craning out the window now, hands braced against the wall beside the window. It's a small bush, but definitely red hemlock.

A tickle on her right wrist makes her look down. It's green. A vine, coiled gently around her wrist, extending all the way to the fig tree in the boys' garden. A climber, by the looks of it. She frowns. How did it stretch this far across their houses? It looks invasive - she'll have to check if it's found its way into her garden.

Then it moves, twitching against her hand, despite the still night. That's strange - has she smoked too much? But witch weed isn't that strong. She must have imagined it. She moves her wrist, planning to pluck the plant off.

The vine at her wrist jerks hard, tightening like a cord suddenly and starts to pull her out the second story window. Her free hand grasps at the basin in panic. She knocks her pipe into the sink and the hand closes over the potion vial instead. Her window springs open completely, and she's lifted, screaming, into the night.

Her throat hurts, but she's no longer in mid air. She's fortunately much closer to the ground. Unfortunately she's in a tree in the West brother's backyard. With no underwear on.

The large fig tree has been overgrown for months. Now there are vines woven through its branches, suspending her low under its canopy. They're wrapped thickly around her waist several times, bunching her dress up. She's perilously close to revealing her lack of underwear, but at least she's safe from falling to her death.

Mercifully, the love potion vial didn't smash against the vines when she was carried in. The potion is a concentrate. It's not something you want to smear on your skin in any volume, although it wouldn't do much, anyway. Love potions only works on sentient beings, so she can't meld with the vine and convince it to let her down.

She's stuck here, waiting for someone to find her. Someone like Bradley West, a gorgeous slice of mage, who is right now taking a shower only a few feet away. Her face burns hot in the cooling night air and she presses her thighs together at the thought of him finding her. The orgasm she had upstairs didn't satisfy her nearly enough, and being tied up reminds her of some of her fantasy scenarios with Brad. She wasn't intending on chasing a man right now, but circumstances have changed.

There's enough ambient light from the surrounding houses to make out details in the garden. The fig tree is in a garden bed against the back fence, hanging over into the vacant lot behind their house. Two more beds line the fences on either side with shrubbery too far beneath her feet for her to reach.

Two of the shrubs closest to her house are red hemlock. It's unmistakable this close, even in the darkness. The rare plant, almost unknown outside witch communities, is here in the mages' backyard. Her stomach flips. If she can convince them to let her have some...

But first she has to get down. She tries to focus. Even brickwork paves the rest of the garden. There's a small standing tin shed tucked along the fence adjoining her house. An ornately wrought dark green table and two matching chairs sit under an awning along the back of the house. It's quaint and vintage. She's been looking for a set like that for months.

Tangled along the awning, and covering the entire back wall of the house, including the door, creep tendrils of vines.

A naked bulb in the back wall of the house lights up, throwing a golden glow into the darkness.

The door handle to the back door turns, and she watches in sudden realization as the vines pull back to allow the door to open, as if driven by their own will. Plants only act like that when they're embedded with a lot of magic, and that means the brothers are vine mages, able to control plants.

She holds her breath.

Through the door steps Lincoln.

Lincoln's blue eyes widen slightly in surprise. Cassia's mouth goes dry. It couldn't be the other one? But she knows she needs to befriend him. Vine mages are a gift from Hecate to a potion making witch. As long as he says nothing too arrogant, it will be fine. She can do this.

"The vines protect us from intruders," he says. "Is there a reason you were on our property line, Ms. Theseira?" A smug smile plays on his lips and it has the same effect as nails on a blackboard.

He's so smug. And still so damn annoyingly pretty. She should control her temper. She really should. But she can't help herself. "I should ask you why your plant assaulted me! I was opening my bathroom window and leaned out too far," she says hotly. "I have no interest in trespassing on your property. Now, if you'll please let me down, I can return to my home."

He looks at her, head cocked to the side. "I'm willing to be neighborly... if you will, too. Do you agree to keep your music at a reasonable volume?"

He folds his arms. He's taken off his jacket, and the outline of his biceps are visible through his white shirt. His gaze scans up her body, only snagging briefly on the hem of her far-too-short dress.

She gets a flash of Brad's naked body in the shower, and pushes it away, feeling heat rise to her face. The vines feel too restrictive around her waist, her thighs too exposed to his inspection.

Under her embarrassment thrums an undercurrent of fear. She's in his backyard, and nobody knows she's here. She needs to stand her ground.

She splutters. "This is not a negotiation! Your... PET... took me out of my home and is holding me against my will."

"It's true. You are now at my mercy. You might want to reconsider that apology," he says, smile dropping as he straightens his cuffs and fiddles with his cufflinks. His suit is different, she realizes. He's in something slightly more formal, with ornate fabric. It's sexy as hell. Her breath quickens.

It's one thing fantasizing about his brother, the younger one with the rebellious vibe. It's another one facing Lincoln - control oozes off him.

She's not really afraid - is she? Her house is right next door. But she knows nothing about this mage, except he's arrogant, entitled, and has moved away from his own kind.

Was it by choice? They could have been thrown out - they could have done anything. She hasn't heard of any rogue murderous mages on the loose, but she's not exactly well connected.

"I'll let you go, Ms. Theseira, as I have a dinner date." Relief floods her. Of course, he has a dinner date, and won't assault her in his backyard. "But as you pointed out, human rules don't apply in the magic world. And since you're the one who trespassed, I think a little time out is in order for you to consider how to be a good neighbor. I'll be back in two hours."

"Wha... what? You can't leave me here!" Before she can say any more, vines wrap around her open mouth, making her choke on the green taste.

"That's better. In case my brother is feeling more sympathetic."

He has a smug little smile on his face before he turns around and walks back into the house.

*Asshole!* She struggles, twisting in the vines, and brings her hands up to tug at the thick strands in her desperation to escape.

The tinkling of glass makes her stomach sink.

The vial in her hand is crushed as the vines tighten, toxic pink goo smearing all over her hands. Her skin burns hot for an instant where the potion touches it, then fades away to nothing. The rest of the goo drips into the cluster of roots at her feet.

She swears against the vines, before they abruptly release her mouth.

She's left panting, inspecting her palms for damage. They're covered in minor cuts. Bright spots of blood ooze into the hot pink goo, but she's otherwise okay. She tries the vines around her waist. They don't budge. Okay.

The love potion shouldn't work on non-sentient creatures, but whatever the mage brothers have done to this plant means the vines might be sentient. And now there's potion in her cuts, and the vines have potion in their roots. The love potion works as a connection, and might already be working in a low grade way. If it works, she might convince it to let her go.

"Hey there... this is all a misunderstanding. If you let me go, I won't be any trouble. I'll just go back home."

She waits. There's no reaction, and she feels foolish. Plants can't think. It must have only the vaguest intelligence, and be blindly obedient to Lincoln.

But there's another option. Now she's not gagged, she can call out and see if the other brother is sympathetic to her position. She has to play this right and convince him to let her down. Her heart jumps foolishly, and she clamps it back down. He could be worse than his brother, no matter how pretty he is. But he's also the key to her freedom.

And somehow, although it might be wishful thinking, she thinks the brothers are quite different.

Regardless, she needs to get down, before that arrogant ass Lincoln comes back. And then she's going to cast a spell so he won't be able to sleep peacefully for a month.

The vine might decide to muffle her again at any moment. She might only get one chance. She breathes in deeply, ready to give it her all.

The cuts on her hand tingles as if in anticipation. Then she screams Brad's name.

# Chapter Four

## BRAD

Brad's drying his hair with a towel when the terrifying banshee scream cuts through the night air. He freezes, listening again, and there it is - screaming. And then, what sounds like his name? He frowns. He heard the front door shut a few minutes ago, so he knows Lincoln has left. The scream sounds like it's coming from the garden.

It could be an intruder. Irene usually acts like a guard vine, but she hasn't been herself. Maybe a mage followed them from Healesville, as if it wasn't enough to make their lives miserable in their own town. Maybe it's another vine mage. He smiles wickedly to himself. Good. The fight in the bar barely scratched the surface of his needs tonight. He'd let a drunk barfly punch him a few times before he knocked the guy out cold. He'd almost felt bad.

In Healesville, fights were easy to find. One of the other mages - one who knew who their birth family was - would start something, and he'd kick their ass. But he'd always let them get at least one punch in before he took them down. It wasn't satisfying without the pain.

The intensity made him feel alive. It was a nice change from the numbness that filled the rest of his life.

He was surprised the first time a girl approached him after a fight, wanting to be fucked in a bathroom stall or up against the back wall of a bar. They wanted a round with the bad boy.

Soon it became routine. Pain then pleasure. A few girls even asked him to hurt them. A part of him was curious about mingling pain with pleasure, but he didn't trust games like that with a casual fuck, and that's all they ever saw him as. It was better to keep things really simple.

Lincoln was the one who liked things complicated - he liked the long game, but always had a string of lovers. Or he did, before their mum died. Now he was more uptight than ever, had cut most of his lovers off, and was obsessed with finding out about their mother's past.

Guess everyone deals in their own way.

Brad bounces on his toes, the adrenalin already kicking in.

He's wearing gray sweats, no shirt, allowing plenty of movement if he has to fight. He grabs a sturdy carving knife from the block in the kitchen before heading to the back door. With one hand on the door handle, he braces himself before stepping outside.

Brad can make any plant in the garden bend to his will, but only Irene, the vine raised by hand by Lincoln and him, will obey them above another vine mage. She's just a plant, but after so many years of being fed with magic, she's as close to sentient as a plant can get. If Irene is out of action and another vine mage is involved, Brad has as much chance as they do of winning this fight.

He turns the handle and lets the door swing open.

The raven-haired witch from next door is strung up in their tree, only a foot or so off the ground. Irene has vines wrapped well around the witch's waist, hiking her dress up to reveal an expanse of brown legs his gaze follows up almost to their root. He tears his eyes up to her face.

She was pretty from afar, from the glimpses he's caught of her in her garden or through a window, but up close, she's downright beautiful. Her light brown eyes are luminous against dark features.

His cock twitches in his sweats. He could get on board with cozying up to witches if they look like this one.

Lincoln wants to find witches to learn more about their mother. Brad doesn't care about who their mother was before she was their mother. He only cares that she died six months ago and they've been picking up the pieces since.

Veering away from the hollow place inside him, his eyes drift to the hem of the witch's dress before catching himself and going back to her face. She's watching him uncertainly. Guilt fills him, but he checks himself against his own embarrassment.

If Irene caught her, the witch was up to something. And the mage community wasn't too happy the brothers left - they were paying a portion of their business as tax to the mage community. She could be a spy, or worse.

His cock will have to wait until he gets some answers.

"Irene, put her down," he says sternly, infusing his voice with his will and magic.

Nothing happens.

He frowns, confused.

"Um hi," the witch says. "I'm Cassia. I leaned too far out my window next door and your pet vine grabbed me." She smiles, as if to emphasize this is all a misunderstanding.

He frowns. "I'm Brad. But you know that - you yelled my name," he says. "Irene wouldn't have grabbed you for crossing into our territory unless she thought you were up to something. So, we're going to get you out of that

tree, and you're going to tell me all about it. Irene, down."
Cassia's face falls, concern creasing her brow.

Nothing happens.

"Um, I don't think she's listening. It really was a misunderstanding. But maybe get me down first and I can explain?"

"I'll get you down, but we don't let thieves off easily in our household. You might prefer Irene's treatment to mine," he says gravely. She looks worried. Hopefully worried enough to tell him what she wants and who she's working with.

He runs a hand through his hair, knife still in the other hand.

He walks closer to her, stepping through the roots of the fig and the vine entangled in it. He holds the knife loosely at his side.

He feels sick at the thought of having to prune Irene, especially after so recently moving. It doesn't hurt her, but it will keep her small and limit her movements, which he knows frustrates her. She's already been unhappy lately. But Lincoln is right - they can't afford to have her go rogue. She has too much of their magic in her, after all these years.

He steps up to the vines wrapped around Cassia, speaking in a soothing voice. Cassia stiffens at his approach, but he doesn't touch her. "Come on then, Irene, enough games. I know you've been stressed with the move, but this is our neighbor. She doesn't mean any harm."

He looks into Cassia's face - she's not looking at him, she's inspecting the surrounding trees. Her heart-shaped face has a doll-like quality, crested by that tangle of black hair. She's a little older than him and looks tired.

As he strokes the vines confining her, Cassia glances at his face as if surprised. A deep flush appears in her cheeks, traveling all the way down her neck into the nape of her black dress. He could reach out and touch the heat of her skin.

The vines don't move. Cassia shakes her head as if frustrated.

"Maybe she'll let you go if you tell me what you want and who you're working with," he suggests.

"I told you, it was an accident," Cassia says stubbornly. "And why would you think I'm working with anyone?"

"Suit yourself," he shrugs. "I can ask you when you're free. After all, I don't want to accidentally hurt Irene while trying to make you talk." She blanches at that. He feels guilty and has to remind himself she's a spy.

He shifts his voice again to soothing. "Now Irene, don't make this difficult." He strokes her vines even more gently now, soothing her with just his fingertips. "Let the nice lady go."

No movement from the vines, but Cassia lets out a soft gasp. He shoots her a sharp look to see if she's in pain, but she won't meet his eye.

He'll have to prune. He knows Irene will grow back, but he hates it. Other vine mages prune their vines regularly, but Lincoln and Brad never have. Lincoln talks tough about discipline, but Brad knows he doesn't have the heart. Maybe that's why Irene's being so difficult now.

He takes a deep breath, steadying himself. Then he lifts the knife.

Cassia lets out a surprised cry as she's jerked abruptly away from him.

# Chapter Five

## CASSIA

When Cassia gets over the sudden movement, she relaxes. Irene is supporting her - she's just a foot further back and up away from Brad, who's right now looking up at her in frustration. He's as gorgeous up close, but far more scary. She's not unhappy about being further away from the knife.

Brad's much taller than she is - and taller than his brother. When he was closer, she noticed his chest was scattered with scars. She's seen the blood on him in the shower. She curses her fantasies for thinking he's sexy. She has no idea what kind of fights he's getting into when he comes home with blood on him - is he in a gang? He could be a killer.

His face had tightened when he talked about finding out the truth about her. Could he have meant it? She was a fool to trust the softness of his features.

Maybe she should just tell him about the red hemlock. She can tell he finds her attractive. Maybe they could trade - something he wants, for something she wants. Her stomach turns at the thought - even in her darkest days in the coven, she never resorted to prostitution. Besides, a trade with a woman for sex might be as abhorrent for him as it is to her - it's not like he would have any shortage of willing women. Maybe he'll get violent if she suggests it. Maybe he'll get violent anyway.

He steps closer, and she realizes she knows nothing about Brad. He's a wild card. At least Lincoln seems civilized and predictable. She didn't think she'd wish Lincoln were still here. She didn't even mind the way Lincoln had looked at her legs. In fact, if she's brutally honest, she liked it.

*Lincoln is strong and caring.*

The voice cuts through Cassia's thoughts, along with a wave of memories and affection. Lincoln's hands gently stroking her. Lincoln's face when he's tending to her roots.

She shakes her head. She doesn't want to feel affection for Lincoln. These are Irene's thoughts, not hers.

Brad murmurs something low and comforting. He strokes Irene's vines. The hair on Cassia's arms stands on end. It's as if Brad's stroking a hand along her own skin. The caress sends a zing straight to her core, pooling a sudden wetness in her core. She presses her legs tightly together.

She's acutely aware of Brad's body, the contours of his naked chest backlit from the porch. His scent is fresh and earthy, like cedarwood and musk.

A memory comes to her that isn't hers. A younger Brad is circled by two mean-faced boys out the front of a neat but run-down suburban home surrounded by a short vine-covered fence. A backpack lies abandoned by him on the pavement. They land one punch, then two, circling him with more blows until he falls on the floor in a ball.

"You should have stayed out of it, half breed," the bigger one says. "Sarah's my girlfriend, and I can say whatever I want to her."

They start kicking, laughing, until Brad grabs the leg of the largest, toppling him over, and punching the other hard in the groin. Blood drips down his nose, but he's laughing through the pain as he drags the boys to his front garden. Irene comes alive from the fence to gag and truss the boys up.

Brad picks up his backpack and walks to the one who spoke. "I can't stop her dating a shit like you. But maybe she won't be so scared of you when everyone hears about you being stuck out here all night. Maybe it'll give her some time to think." Then he walks inside.

Cassia feels Irene's surge of pride at the memory.

*Bradley is kind and giving. He deserves love.*

A suggestion - a mental push - and a vision of Brad and Cassia entwined within the vines, bodies joined in ecstasy. She stifles a gasp and can't meet Brad's eyes. He's stepped closer - he's so close now he could lean over and kiss her.

A flash of light close to her draws her attention. He's still holding the knife.

The vines jerk her back abruptly. She gasps at the tightness and pushes aggressively at the vines at her waist.

"Let me go, you bitch!" she yells, pounding on the surrounding vines. Tendrils snake out of the tree above her, lifting her hands above her head, binding them.

*Stop struggling. Bradley won't hurt you.*

Cassia knows Irene believes that's true. And after her vision of Brad's past she believes it too. But she's not so sure about the pornographic images Irene's been showing her. Sure, Brad is hot, and not the serial killer she was starting to suspect. But she still prefers her sex more on the consensual side.

"Irene, you will obey me," Brad says, stepping forward with knife in hand.

The vines pulled Cassia back further into the tree. She can feel Irene's defiance. At this rate, they could play this cat-and-mouse game until Lincoln comes home.

*Lincoln deserves love too.*

Irene's thought pushes through, much to Cassia's irritation. She won't be some surrogate sex puppet for Irene's admiration of these boys.

Brad swears and presses his lips into a determined line. He swipes at Irene's vines. Cassia feels a stab of loss as a thick vine falls to the floor, but her binds don't move. Irene isn't in pain, but there's a sadness coming through their connection. Brad is hurting her. He doesn't understand she wants to help him - to help them both. He's been so sad lately. Images of Brad coming home bloody and ragged, or lying in bed for days at a time, flash through Cassia's head.

*You want him too, tell him witch.*

Brad cuts another thick vine. His mouth is pressed in a determined line, tension emanating off him.

Suddenly, she can feel him. His frustration at the situation, his worry about Irene's strange behavior. Underlying that is a fear that he'll have to uproot Irene - destroy her completely.

Cassia feels sick with all his anxieties flowing into her. Feeling him directly is more convincing than any memory Irene could show her. Brad won't hurt her, and he hates the thought of harming Irene. His level of concern is dizzying. Cassia can't remember the last time anyone cared about her as much as Brad cares about this plant.

She swears. "Stop," she says. She's tired of pulling her wrists against the vines and falls limp.

"Irene's not crazy. I had a love potion and spilled some on us. It seems to be working like a mind melding. She's... confused." She doesn't mention how much she's getting from Brad directly.

"You're mind melded?" he asks. He steps forward again, knife still in hand. Worry tugs at his mouth. "It must be a pretty powerful potion to work on a plant."

"Yeah, it is," Cassia says bitterly, remembering there's none left. "But that's what's happening here. And it means I can feel what Irene is feeling. There's no point in cutting more of her. She won't let me go or let you get close until you drop the knife."

He drops the knife without hesitation. "Is Irene okay?" he asks. "She hasn't been the same since we moved." A surge of homesickness comes through the connection. A memory of being weak, and building strength, sending roots deep into the earth.

"She's... homesick. But she's better now."

"Good." He pauses. "But that doesn't explain about you." His voice is low, dangerous. He thinks she's working with someone. The brothers must have someone after them. Through their connection, she feels he doesn't want to hurt her - but he will if it means protecting his brother and himself. Panic flutters in her chest. She needs to convince him she's harmless - even if that means confessing things she'd rather not.

*Tell him, witch.*

The vines around Cassia's waist tighten at the mental push. An alien memory from Irene - Cassia stalking Irene's territory, Irene's family. Eyeing Brad when he was most vulnerable. Irene had watched Cassia's orgasm with dispassionate curiosity. But then reacted with shuddering alarm - inhuman but still recognisable - when Cassia leaned out past the boundary fence between the two houses.

"That doesn't make me a thief," Cassia thinks indignantly, hoping Irene can hear.

*You trespassed. Tell him or I leave you here.*

Irene's rules were black and white. Trespassing activated her protective instincts. Looks like she has no choice. "I was... I saw the red hemlock in your garden," Cassia says, tugging against the binds at her wrists to distract herself from his gaze. "Up there," she nods her head at her bathroom window. "I need the hemlock for a spell and it's really hard to find. I leaned too far out the window and that's why I'm in your backyard. Your guard dog isn't broken. I wasn't going to steal from you, but I did cross your boundary."

He frowns. "Okay." He steps forward. Irene doesn't pull her back this time. "So why isn't she letting you go now?"

"Your brother found me and decided I deserved to stay here until he got back from dinner," Cassia admits, her look darkening. "He's a real charmer."

*Stop lying.*

The vines tighten around her wrists, and a new vine ropes its way around her neck. She winces, lifting her neck to accommodate for the sudden necklace.

Brad's eyes narrow. "What are you leaving out?"

"She's... your pet is a vine, okay? The love potion is not supposed to work with a sentient plant because they're not supposed to exist. I..."

Cassia stops. There is no way she's telling Brad she was watching him in the shower. The vines around her waist and wrist tighten painfully. She gasps.

"Okay!" she bursts out. The vines relax marginally, but quiver in warning. "I... you leave your window open, okay? Like wide open. I saw you in the shower. She's interpreting that without a lot of filters."

She doesn't look at Brad's face. She hopes never to look at Brad's face again.

"You were watching me?" he asks, voice teasing. The tension at having him this close shifts quickly, zinging excitement into her core. Now she's felt the edges of his thoughts, he isn't so scary.

Leaves brush against her thighs and her throat hitches. They're grazing on the edge of her skirt, close to her most sensitive places. Irene wants Cassia ripe for him.

There's triumph coming from Irene now, and Cassia resents it even as she lifts her eyes to meet Brad's. His eyes are intense on her, focused on her lips. Her skin feels more sensitive under his gaze, her nipples tight against her dress. She has to take control of this situation.

Leaves graze the lips of her wetness, and she closes her eyes and groans instead.

# Chapter Six

## BRAD

When Cassia says they're mind melded, Brad reaches for his connection with Irene. Usually it's a one-way street - his will, or Lincoln's, and her response. But this time, he listens, and he can feel Cassia - sense her through the connection. He can feel the intensity of her arousal as Irene's leaves brush her thighs, the wet lips between her legs. She closes her eyes and groans.

His cock comes to attention. He fights his arousal to keep his thinking straight.

There's no sense that she's been sent to harm them. He can feel the truth in her words. The old community might not even be after them, although Lincoln is always paranoid about it. She really was after the red hemlock, a pretty flower their mother liked. And she had been watching him in the shower.

He can smell her desire - sweet and salty. It makes his mouth water.

But he has to hear the words.

"What would you like me to do to you, Cassia? I don't play games - I want a woman to tell me what she wants." He runs a finger lightly over her cheek, watching her expression as her eyes flutter open. She opens her mouth, her eyes falling to his lips. Desires pulses through their connection.

He leans in and the vines around her neck release. He takes her chin in his hands and presses his mouth to hers softly. She tastes like smoke and very faintly, like strawberries.

He waits for her to kiss him back, letting her set the pace. It doesn't take long for her mouth to grow hungry, tongue darting out to lick along his lips. He opens his mouth, gladly letting her in.

He's used to women being hungry for him, and he can faintly smell witch weed on her breath. This should feel like every casual fuck he's ever had. But somehow it doesn't.

Love potions are commonly used amongst magic users to enhance lovemaking, but none of his flings has ever lasted long enough to experiment with them. Maybe that's what this is - intimacy. Not earned, but a shortcut. He can feel Cassia's sweetness, her loneliness, her independence, and her trust in him. Despite being tied up against her will, she wants him. In fact she wants him more because of it.

Some foolish part of him hopes it's because she can sense as much about him as he does about her. He's glad she's tied up, because he feels more vulnerable right now than he has in any fistfight.

He presses her to his chest. The vines free her arms and suddenly her hands are all over him, running along his shoulders as if she's reveling in the shape of him.

When he pulls away, they're both gasping, foreheads leaning together as they recover. And his cock is aching for release.

"Well, she let part of you go," he says, smiling. She says nothing, breathing hard, her arms still on his back. "She hasn't let you go completely yet, though," he says. And he knows why. Through the connection, he can feel Cassia throb with need. She's on fire, and Irene won't let her go until she's satisfied. "What else can I do to help with that?" he asks, voice rough.

She bites down on her lip before answering. He can feel her hesitation warring with her body's need. He stays still, letting her lead this time. "Touch me," she says breathlessly. Their bodies press together, but he feels vines gently brush his shoulders, and he steps back.

Vines wind into the collar of her dress and skim the bottom of her skirt. A sharp ripping sound rents the air, and perfectly formed small breasts spill out of her new neckline, dark nipples like hard pebbles. The hem of her skirt is lifted gently, revealing a neatly trimmed pussy, glistening wet with desire.

He swallows, eyes devouring her for a moment before he steps in to assist.

His mouth dips to her right breast, taking a nipple into his mouth while his left hand pinches the other. He dips his free hand between her legs. A groan escapes from her lips as he strokes her wetness as gently as he stroked Irene's limbs earlier.

Her body stiffens, moans becoming more urgent as she writhes against him, fingernails scraping along his back.

Frustration leaks through their connection. She wants more of him. He pinches her nipple harder, biting the other. She writhes against him.

On instinct, he pulls back, gaze taking in her needy body before locking eyes with her. For a heartbeat, she meets his eyes in silence as he withdraws the friction she's been begging for. Despite the attraction between them, and the melded connection, he sees in her eyes the apprehension at screwing a stranger she's just met.

So he says, "This is a pretty good way to say hello."

She scoffs a laugh, but looks at him uncertainly. Through their connection, vulnerability pulses, giving him the courage to say, "Maybe we can try for dinner before the bondage next time, Cassia."

She laughs louder this time. She doesn't have to say yes. He kisses her more gently, just a touch of the lips. He wonders at their softness, even as his hand slides down to rub against her clitoris again at a slower speed. She whimpers, and he keeps going until her breath comes in gasps.

He pulls back again to meet her eyes as he pushes a finger slowly inside her. He's not sure why he needs to look at her again, but it feels right, and he enjoys the helpless lust in her eyes as he pumps in and out, drawing his finger all the way past her clit. When he moves to two fingers he's gratified by a full body shudder and a hot wetness flooding his hand.

At three fingers she comes. He feels it through his fingers as she clenches around him, through the shaking in her body, and the rough cry she gives at the explosion. And he feels it through their connection. Her crescendo feels like reaching the top of a rollercoaster and touching the sky. Suspended in ecstasy, mind blank white with pleasure, and a sense of complete rightness with the world. Afterwards she collapses in a happy fog.

Goddam. If he felt that every time he came he'd never have to fight again. He keeps his arms wrapped around her, above the vines that still bind her. She settles softly into his arms, spent.

His cock is so hard it's almost painful, but it's been a long time since he's made a woman come like that. In fact, he might have never made a woman come like that. He wants to stay in this space forever.

He feels Irene's interest at the strange sensations coming from Cassia's body. The pleasure isn't hers, but she's enjoying being a passenger.

Vines wave tendrils across Cassia's shoulders, as if soothing her in the orgasm's aftermath.

Cassia blinks in wonder. "I can feel you," she whispers, and smiles. Her eyes look down at the erection clearly tenting his sweats. She clears her throat. "And I'm still in these vines. I think maybe Irene expects some quid pro quo." She grins this time, and starts to kneel. Brad helps her, and the vines loosen.

When she's on her knees atop a soft blanket of vines that appears under her, he steps out of his sweats. His erection springs into the cool night air, pre-cum already beading the tip.

She raises her head and licks the end of his cock. Through his connection with Irene, he feels Cassia's desire to please him, to watch his pleasure. She takes more and more of him into her mouth. When he feels the softness in the back of her throat, on the head of his cock, he groans. She tugs gently on his balls, his mind goes blank.

His orgasm crashes through him, unexpected and intense. He cries out in release. Black dots dance in front of his eyes. He reaches a hand out blindly to rest against a branch of the fig tree stretching above him. She keeps suckling on him, swallowing him down.

He's still recovering, but through his haze he notices the vines around Cassia's waist are unraveling. He tries not to feel too smug about obviously satisfying her needs, when a voice cuts through his pleasure.

"Don't stop on my account," Lincoln says dryly.

The vines around Cassia's waist tighten, and she's yanked back up and away from both of them, her arms above her head.

# Chapter Seven

# CASSIA

A searing hatred for Lincoln flashes through Cassia's mind. It temporarily overwhelms the humiliation at being trussed up in a tree naked. She wriggles against the new vines at her waist, but they won't budge. She can't cover her breasts, and her juices are dripping down her legs from Brad's attentions.

Lincoln isn't looking at her though - he's averting his eyes, lips pressed together in irritation.

"Dammit, Lincoln!" Brad says, pulling his sweats on.

Cassia wonders how Brad is going to explain this, but she's glad someone else is doing the talking. She's still patching her mind back together after the floating bliss of their sex.

"Irene's mind melded with Cassia, and Irene wouldn't let go until Cassia was... satisfied. Irene was letting go before you walked in."

Lincoln's eyes flick towards her now, grazing lightly over her body before turning back to his brother. She's not sure if she's humiliated, angry or...

*You like it when Lincoln looks at you.*

She shoves Irene's thoughts away and pushes back all her own rage and shame. She feels Irene's confusion. Well, Irene isn't the only one. Cassia's libido has always been high. That's why her coven sent one of the most attractive boys of her generation to screw her over. It's embarrassing that it worked and embarrassing that her determination to swear off all men has lasted such a short time.

"It seemed like you were getting more satisfied than she was," Lincoln says in a dry tone.

Brad runs a hand through his hair, looking irate and a little sheepish. "Irene was letting go. But she pulled her back when you got home."

They both turn to look at Cassia. She freezes, and remembers that despite the intimacy she just shared with Brad, she barely knows these boys.

Lincoln continues icily, gaze fixed on her. "Perhaps the pretty witch would like me to watch?" His lip curls into a smirk. A rush of heat fills her body, and a familiar rustling comes from the surrounding vines.

Vines wrap around her ankles, dragging them apart. She gasps at the sudden exposure, before vines wrap around her neck and mouth, gagging her.

"Jesus Irene," Brad says. "That's enough, let Cassia go."

Brad steps to block Cassia's naked sex from Lincoln's gaze. Lincoln frowns and looks away, but Cassia didn't miss the hunger in his eyes when he looked at her.

She must be blushing from tip to toe, but she feels Irene's pleasure at Lincoln's hungry stare, and the unmistakable tenting in his dress pants.

But this isn't like it was with Brad. Lincoln doesn't like her, doesn't respect her. Her desire for him is out of place with his disregard for her. Lincoln might want her body, but he'll go back to treating her like something under his shoe as soon as this is over.

She doesn't want this. She lets all her humiliation rise to the surface, feeding it with the sense of every rejection she's ever had - every lie a man has told her to get in her pants. That's all his erection means.

She knows Brad and Lincoln can probably feel it all - can feel every humiliation from a man in her life - but she can't help that. She needs to get through to Irene.

"Irene, put her down," Lincoln barks sharply. Irene trembles. Obeying Lincoln is embedded into her core. But now she feels Cassia's perspective of him. The vines around Cassia's ankles, wrists, neck and mouth slowly unwind. Cassia sighs in relief and adjusts her dress to cover her breasts loosely. But the vines at her waist don't release.

*You should be ashamed of yourself*, Irene shoots to Lincoln.

He looks genuinely shocked.

*Lincoln is good*, Irene continues through their connection to all of them. Cassia gets flashes of Lincoln at a dying woman's bedside, then in his office, late into the night.

*Explain to her you're good, Lincoln.*

"Irene, that's enough," Lincoln sighs.

*I won't let her go until you explain.* A stubborn wave shoots through the connection.

"Brad, are Irene and Cassia's thoughts more clear to you now than they were initially?"

Brad frowns, then nods. "Yes. At first it was faint. Now it feels stronger."

"And Irene would never dream of openly defying me. Mind melds with really powerful potions can last days, and they're stronger with contact. But if you break the connection too soon, the trauma could cause permanent damage."

Worry cuts through Cassia's embarrassment. Lincoln's right, and he doesn't even know how strong the love potion is. It's the strongest one she's ever seen - a family secret passed to her by her mother. She died when Cassia was young, and Cassia was the only one in the coven who could master the tricky spell. Not only that, but Cassia improved it - or at least, that's what she thought she'd done. Or maybe all love potions act this wacky when they're used in high concentration with sentient plants.

Some of the girls in her coven stole the potion from her mother once and took it themselves. Their families didn't know and separated them. The girls were in a coma for a week, and there was real fear they might end up catatonic. There's no getting around it. She could be stuck with Irene for weeks.

*Explain,* Irene pushes again, and the leaves around her shake in agitation.

"I can't get to know the woman with her stuck up in a tree like a prisoner," Lincoln says coolly. "Perhaps you could let our guest go and we can get to know each other better."

Cassia feels Irene hesitate.

"Cassia is worth more than sex in a tree, Irene," Brad says gently. Cassia feels her face warm when he looks at her.

She can't meet his eyes for too long. She's still processing what happened before Lincoln interrupted them. She can see Lincoln's eyes flicking over the both of them, but she doesn't have time for his assessment.

The intimacy with Brad was... intense. Sex with a love potion is only better if you're completely aligned to your lover, and Brad and her had a connection she's never felt before. But isn't that exactly what she felt with the last boyfriend who screwed her over? And all the ones before that?

Lincoln cuts through her swirling thoughts. "I can't explain like a savage in the wild. Ms. Theseira, would you like to join me for a cup of tea inside? We can talk in a more civilized fashion." He bows at Cassia, his eyes fixed on hers as if to say 'help me out here.'

"Yes, I... I would rather like that," Cassia says. She forces herself to imagine a soothing cup of tea, and Brad and Lincoln and her smiling at one another over a kitchen table. The vines at her waist loosen. Brad looks hopeful, and Lincoln holds still.

Cassia tries to keep her body relaxed as the vines unravel, and she steps away from the tree. One step goes smoothly, as does the second. The third, however... she tugs on the ankle, which has a vine wrapped tightly around it, stopping her from going further.

"Won't you join us inside, Ms. Theseira? We'll lead the way," Lincoln says, and gestures for Brad to go inside ahead of him.

They both head inside, and Cassia feels the tension on her ankle loosen. The vine is still there, but she can walk freely, still attached to Irene. She has to hand it to Lincoln. He knew what he was doing when talking to the plant. She could function almost completely like this, if Irene extended enough to let her move around her house.

She follows the boys inside, thinking maybe she's wrong about Lincoln. He didn't seek to take advantage of her situation, and she can feel his care for Irene despite his icy demeanor. And she knows he can see something's going on between her and Brad - something more than sex. Strangely, she senses he approves.

# CHAPTER EIGHT

# LINCOLN

The air is warmer inside their house, and under the smoke in his nostrils it smells faintly of hot food and fresh flowers.

"Get the kettle on, will you, Brad?" Lincoln asks, keeping his voice light as he steps into his study. He looks behind them - as expected, Irene has let the witch follow. "Please follow Brad into the kitchen, Ms. Theseira. I'll be right with you."

"Call me Cassia, please," she says, as she follows. She's adjusting her clothing, as if he didn't see everything she covered up a few minutes ago. Still, it will make it easier to concentrate. He leaves Brad to host while he goes to his study.

Within the walls of his private space, his thoughts roam. He's getting impressions of Cassia and Brad through the connection with Irene, and he has no doubt they're getting impressions of him. With a wall between them, the sensations should be more faint. Besides, with the way those two are looking at each other, they're hardly thinking about him.

Irene's intervention was unexpected, but he had already been thinking about Cassia all night. His other lead, Vera, didn't show up to dinner. She probably remembered her allegiance to her husband, he thinks bitterly. They had been lovers for a month now despite that, and Vera was his main chance to connect to the witch world. The other one had just been trussed up, naked, in his backyard.

Witches notoriously hate mages, only dealing with them for useful trade between the species. Since the West brothers have no further ties with the mage world, they're useless to coven witches. He was banking on Vera's fondness for him, or at least the pleasure he provided her.

When Vera didn't show up, his mind had turned to Cassia. In fact, he'd been having trouble not thinking of her, trussed up temptingly in the garden. Cassia obviously wanted something, and that gave him leverage. He had rushed to come home.

Finding her with Brad had shocked him - and made him jealous. Cassia was a vision - like a goddess, wanton and unashamed, vines wrapped around her, taking his brother deep down her throat.

And then he felt her through his connection with Irene. He can feel it even now. She wants Brad, yes. But she also wants Lincoln, physically, even while she shrinks from him. She's worried he'll reject her. He could laugh out loud.

Brad and he had girlfriends in the mage world, but they weren't considered a good prospect because they were only half mage. The boys were the dirty little secret, the forbidden fruit. So Lincoln leaned into the identity. He fulfilled women's filthiest desires, while fully knowing they weren't equals in real life. He was the half breed, the man they would screw for a good time before they found a suitable husband.

Maybe Cassia will be the same. But he doesn't think so. He reaches tenuously through their connection through Irene. The link is still strong - the spell must be potent for it to last this long.

He's accustomed to the mutual pleasure love potions provide. But this connection is stronger - this potion feels like more than your average love potion. And Cassia feels like no other woman he's ever felt before. She's different.

Her lust is wild, untamed, and deeply hungry. And under that hunger, loneliness. She's searching for connection in any way she can, but also fighting her own desire for it. She wants to belong, but she wants to make her own way. He understands, because it's a struggle that echoes his own. She can see why Brad and he have found kinship in each other.

They can help each other - and she'll help them when she knows them better, he's sure of it. If he can get past the walls she's built to protect herself. If he can convince her, they could work together.

Now he understands her more, he can see how badly he came across at her doorstep. She's been wounded deeply, and he triggered her defenses. He did that - him and his pride, his big mouth.

He needs to make her see they're not so different, even though they're half mages and she's a witch. He realizes he's standing still, staring at the wall, lost in thought. Well, there has been a lot to process. And there will still be more.

He grabs the grimoire and takes it into the kitchen.

Brad raises his eyebrows when he sees the grimoire. He's carrying a cup of tea towards Cassia, who's sitting at their kitchen table, eyes roaming the room. Lincoln feels a pang of pride in his chest at the way her eyes take in their home.

When she sees him, her expression becomes wary. It hurts him to see. She's relaxed, with Brad. But he's given her no reason to feel comfortable.

Her eyes widen when he puts the book in front of her.

"Our adopted mother's," he explains. "We were raised amongst mages, but she was never accepted in that community because of her blood. She took us in because we weren't accepted either. We're only half mages - the result of dalliances with normies. Brad and I were both illegitimate, and family ties are everything to mages. In their eyes we were tainted." He lets some of the hurt of that leak into their connection. He sees her eyes soften in realization, feels it through their connection.

"She turned her back on witchcraft completely. She died recently. We were going to ask if you could help. We would pay you, of course - to translate, and teach us about our mother. But you didn't seem to like me very much," he adds lightly.

"Well, you are a jerk," she points out.

"He really is," Brad agrees, his back leaning against the kitchen counter, hands cupping his own cup of tea. He hasn't bothered putting a shirt on, which Lincoln is trying not to be irritated by.

He shifts his attention back to Cassia. She may still reject him. She has every right. But she reaches for the grimoire. His heart leaps with hope.

She flicks through the book, and stops on the title page. "This is from my coven!" she says with shock. "There's a coven symbol engraved on the first page - see?" She turns the book to show us. "It's a three headed snake in a circle. The family should be on the next page, but it's been ripped out." A furrow appears on her brow as she studies it, her finger tracing the edge of the missing page as Lincoln has so often done.

Lincoln's heart leaps in his chest. The synchronicity surprises him - and more, delights him. And maybe it's her excitement that causes his heart to leap, and the thought of having her close.

"We haven't been able to read it," Lincoln says. He comes closer, but she doesn't react, lost in the book. "When Brad and I look, it's only blank pages."

He leans over her shoulder. He breathes in her sweet scent - strawberries and musk. It makes him feel - strange. Nostalgic for something he's never had.

Brad watches them curiously. Not jealous - of course, he has no need to be. Cassia is obviously his. Acceptance settles in the pit of Lincoln's stomach. Cassia is exactly what Brad needs, and he's happy for his brother. So there's no reason to stand further away from her.

Meanwhile Cassia has synchronized so completely with Irene, Lincoln can feel her curiosity in the dusty pages through their connection. Curiosity with an undercurrent of excitement. He lets the connection guide his next words.

"We don't have the connections to entice a coven witch to help, but if you came from the same coven as our mother, we really need you, Cassia," he says. "Will you help us?"

She looks up at him in surprise. Her eyes are wide, and in them he can see her doubt, and her fear. Her eyes flick to his lips, and he feels her lust sear through to him before she quickly clamps it down. His heart leaps in surprised response. She flushes scarlet and closes the book.

Brad continues to watch them warily, face neutral. Lincoln feels for more in their connection, but they're both accustomed to hiding their emotions from the other through Irene's connection.

"Um, well, actually... I'd love to read this grimoire. My mother died in a fire when I was young and her grimoire was lost. So I would help you, anyway." Her eyes drift away from his when she talks about her mother. "But um... I was in your garden for a reason," she says, licking her lips, eyes darting back towards him.

"I have a business - gifts, themed around love. At the heart of each one is the love potion that merged Irene and me. And I need red hemlock flowers to make the potion. My old coven isn't happy about the competition, so they're blocking my suppliers. I'm happy to trade you red hemlock for information on the coven your mother came from."

He extends a hand for her to shake. "It's a deal," he says. "We can provide you with as much red hemlock as you need." Real relief floods her face, and his stomach flips slightly. He's been in business for long enough to realize she desperately needs their help. He could have pushed for more, but he somehow still feels like he won.

"We also understand our home community trying to hold us back," Brad says. "Our town wasn't too happy we were taking our business elsewhere."

"What do you do?" Cassia asks.

"Witch weed," Brad says. "We figured out the effects work mildly with humans as well, so we sell natural highs. The other mages looked down on the trade, saw it as a cheap use of our growing talent, but they soon changed their tune once the profits started rolling in."

Lincoln watches him with surprise. This is chattier than Brad's been in months. Cassia will be good for him, he realizes. Despite her surprising attraction to Lincoln. He vows to stay away for his brother's sake.

Brad continues, "Our online trade really makes the money, though. It doubled our profits. Completely legal, packaged and delivered straight to the client."

Brad is the tech savvy one in their business relationship, while Lincoln handles the money and other logistics. But lately Brad's been barely keeping on top of things.

"That's the unfortunate thing about traditional covens. They're deeply suspicious of technology. I wouldn't know where to start with a website," Cassia says.

"Brad will be happy to teach you," Lincoln interrupts. "Since you'll be staying with us for a while. Because of the mind meld, of course."

Cassia looks at him in surprise. "I thought... I mean, I'm just next door, so Irene could extend..." He feels her shock reverberate through their connection.

"She won't extend that far, unfortunately," Brad says. "She's still adjusting to the move. In our old place, yes, but it will be months before she can stretch that far. I'm surprised she could reach your window."

"We can't force you to stay," Lincoln adds, with regret. "But you are aware of the risks of separation, given the depth of the connection. You could be traumatized if we try to break it off now, or in worst-case scenarios, lobotomized."

She puts the grimoire down on the table, fingers lingering on the cover, mouth pressed in a tight line. "This is a more powerful potion. It could take days to separate."

"We have a spare room," Brad says, not doing a good job of hiding his happiness at her staying.

"I have orders to fulfill," she says.

"You can make them here," Brad says. "We don't use the kitchen much, anyway."

"We can fetch whatever you need from your house," Lincoln says. "Including some new clothes." She looks down and pulls together the edges of her ripped dress, as if suddenly realizing what she's wearing. "If you make a list, I can fetch what you need." He hands her a paper and pen he had ready in his back pocket.

A spike of irritation flows through their connection. "What?" he asks.

"You could pretend to be upset that I'm stuck here," she says. "I know you're keen to learn more about your mother, but this compromises my freedom," she says tartly. "You could be less of a twat about it."

Brad snickers from across the room.

Lincoln feels his face heat. He's used to being direct, and asking for what he wants, and then living with disappointment if he doesn't get it. Cassia is different - he can feel she wants him on some level, but if he's too direct, she'll pull away. And as usual, Brad gets away with his happiness at having her stay, while Lincoln does not. "I'm... sorry. I'll pretend to be more regretful. While we get your things, you can take a shower if you like, and maybe borrow some less... torn clothing."

Cassia stares at him. He stands, stiffly. He can't get anything through the connection. Brad snickers again.

"Well, I suppose that'll do," Cassia says finally, and takes the pen and paper and writes. Through their connection, he senses a smile.

# CHAPTER NINE

## BRAD

B rad sees Cassia into the bathroom and gets her a towel from under the sink. "I'll get you some warm clothes, okay? Take a shower, I'll knock when I come back. If you don't answer I'll leave them by the door."

He half closes the door to give her some space, leaving a gap for the vine twining to her ankle, and heads to his own room. He passes Lincoln's closed bedroom door, hearing Lincoln's ensuite shower already running.

Brad enters his bedroom and crashes onto his back, willing his erection to ebb. It started up again while they were in the kitchen. He liked having her there. There aren't many women who've been in his space before.

The decor in his own room is sparse. The only furniture is a small wooden bookshelf holding some dog-eared paperbacks, a speaker that connects to his phone, a necklace and four or five ceramic cats that belonged to his mother. One wall is a mirrored door that holds a built-in wardrobe - a new addition on the original design of the house.

His mattress sits on a plain wooden bedframe. Draped over everything, emerging from large white pots in three of the corners, are creeping vines. There are three different varieties, all capable of flowering when the air needs refreshing, but at the moment they're a tangle of greenery, giving the air a crisp but earthy scent.

He prefers to keep things simple - he's not sure how long he's sticking around for.

He knows Lincoln wants him to stay, but the business is Lincoln's baby. Brad hasn't figured out what his own thing is yet except fuck and fight. He hated Healesville - the only thing that made it bearable was their mother. Now the bandaid has been ripped off, he could go anywhere, do anything.

His mind drifts back to the witch. She's left her people too, her coven. Like his mother - he knows so little about the witch communities and their lifestyle - his mother didn't want to talk about it.

His mother. The pit of his stomach drops out when he thinks of her - the grief is always there, ready to swallow him whole. The numbness is better, safer. Or better yet, the delicious escape he felt tonight.

He's pretty sure it's just an escape, anyway. A very, very intense escape. The best he's ever had, in fact.  He hasn't felt that kind of connection for a long time. He hasn't let himself get that close. But it felt right.

He'd like more than just a release, and he gets enough from their connection to think maybe she would too. But he can see Lincoln's interest in her, and he feels an attraction coming from her end towards Lincoln too. He's not too sure how he feels about that.

In Healesville, women sought them out - one or both of them - for a reason. They saw Brad because they wanted to piss off their parents or brothers, and mark themselves wild enough. They saw Lincoln in secret, to wring the last from their youth before settling down to a more suitable life than the West brothers could offer. It was Lincoln's women who usually asked for a guest star in the bedroom.

They'd shared women a handful of times, but never women they cared about, and those women never stuck around for long. Who's he kidding? None of his girls ever stuck around for long. Healesville was a pretty small dating pool and he wasn't considered stick around material.

He got used to it and didn't expect more. But it got tiring.

It feels different with Cassia, even with Lincoln involved. Maybe because of Irene's connection, or because she's sober. Maybe because she's beautiful.

Whatever the reason, he wants her to meet his eyes more than he wants to fuck her. He can still feel her hesitation, the uncertainty running through her since she was let down from the tree.

He has to remember that none of tonight has been strictly consensual. They haven't even had penetrative sex yet, and they're still weirdly connected through Irene. She needs some time and space. And then she can choose what she wants to do next. He hopes she chooses him. The thought surprises him. Tonight is full of surprises.

He reaches out to Irene. She's happy - smug, almost, her vines extending around the house to cover the sides as well as the back. She's still connected to Cassia through the mind meld, although the connection isn't nearly as strong now.

He gets a flash of sensation - hot water hitting overly sensitive nipples, running across every part of her skin. Cassia in the shower. His cock hardens again, and he reaches out to palm himself through his sweats. Flashes of sensation come through from her - shame, confusion, determination, competing with the singing in her body - a longing that echoes deeply through his core.

*Fuck this.* He gets out of bed, grabs some sweats and a t-shirt, and walks down the hall to the bathroom.

# Chapter Ten

# CASSIA

In the bathroom, Cassia takes a moment to collect herself. It's strange being in a room she's looked into so many times. Their bathroom is more modern than hers - the original vintage charm replaced by slick black-and-white tiles, a nod to art déco.

The shower takes up the left side of the room, with no curtain blocking it from her window on the right. She can see right out into her bathroom window from the shower or the basin beside it.

Brad could have turned around and looked up at any time and seen her watching him. Maybe that's what she was hoping for, secretly. But nothing from her fantasies could top what they did tonight.

Sitting in the window is a pot plant of pothos ivy, extending tendrils across most of the surrounding wall.

She watches it closely for any movement, but it seems to be non-sentient.

She steps into the shower and turns on the hot water, hoping it will blast away her... whatever's going on. Lust? Excitement? Relief? Maybe a bit of everything. Irene keeps a tendril of connection on her ankle, but it's not painful. She's almost getting used to it, even if it is disarming to have her emotional and mental state transmitted to three other sentient beings.

Her mind drifts to the grimoire. She tried to suppress her excitement, but she's never read an old grimoire from her coven. Her mother's was their family grimoire, and it's taboo to read another family's grimoire. The coven would have thrown her out for the offense, and no witch would respect her. She feels a stab of guilt at reading the one the boys have, but they can't read the grimoire themselves, so she's helping them out.

It is exciting though. Spells are specific to families, and many only exist in the grimoire. Her mother's love spell is the only one she knows, because her mother shared it with the coven before she died. So it's unlikely any of the spells she reads in the boys' grimoire would work for her. But some might. She could figure out what family the grimoire belonged to, also... but maybe after she's read it, of course.

She would help them even if they couldn't help her, though. She can feel the sharpness of their grief when they mention their mother. It reminds her of her own loss, even though she was only three when her mother was caught in the burning shed. It still hurt to have lost her only family. Raised by the coven but nobody in particular, she bounced from house to house and never really felt like she belonged anywhere.

The hot water washes away the old grief, and she runs her hands over her body, bringing her back to more recent events, and a flush of heat in her face.

What must Brad think of her and their scene in the backyard? Never mind Lincoln - She can't bring herself to care about what he thinks right now. What does Lincoln even like in a woman? He's so arrogant, so sanctimonious. *So sexy*, her thoughts betray her. But not her type, obviously. She likes men who are less complicated, like Brad.

She thinks of the naked desire on Brad's face in the garden. It was like a warm bath after everything that had happened with Darren, calming something inside her.

She focuses on the delicious feeling of being with Brad. Her fear that he'd harm her quickly fading. It was Lincoln who made her uncertain, Lincoln who got under her skin like sandpaper. Lincoln was annoying, but Brad emanated naked lust... She could see it in his face, feel it in his touch, and through Irene's connection.

Her nipples harden in the water, and she rubs her hands quickly over her body, sloughing away the slickness between her legs.

She shakes her head, ducking her head under the spray and making the water hotter. There's shampoo and conditioner two-in-one in the shower, so she squeezes some into her hand and lathers it into her hair. Clean is good. Heat is good. It might distract her from the singing aftermath in her body. That was one hell of an orgasm Brad gave her and had left her clenching on nothing.

And to think, she'd been looking at Brad's cock in this very shower earlier today. And then had it in her mouth only moments ago! In theory, it was under the coercion of Irene, but Cassia knew she could have made Irene stop at any time, if she hadn't desired Brad quite so much. He was exactly her type - dangerous, sexy, and bad news.

She can tell he gets in fights for the rush, chasing an escape. It wasn't so different from her with sex, when she was younger. But the escape was only temporary.

She turns the water off. Touching her naked body, even to clean it, isn't helping. She rubs the towel over herself vigorously, wrapping it around herself tightly, and picks up her dress. Brad was going to bring her clothes, but she can't wait. She needs to be clothed. She puts the towel on the sink and pulls her ripped dress on.

There's a firm knock on the door. She sucks in a breath and uses one hand to close the neck of her dress. With the other, she opens the door. Brad's knuckles are poised to knock again, a bundle of clothes in his other arm.

He grins at her wickedly through a flop of dark hair, eyes glittering. It's a grin full of mischief, but also kindness. And of course, he's not wearing a shirt. He hasn't put one on yet tonight. She could reach out and trace the lines of his tattoos. She stops breathing.

He walks into the bathroom, puts the bundle of clothes on the sink, and turns to face her.

"Brought you some spare clothes. My turn in the shower then, unless you wanna watch with a better view?" He's casual now, as if sensing her apprehension and giving her space to decide.

"I... should go to sleep," she stammers out.

"Sure," he says. "Like I said, we have a spare room. With an internal lock. And no plants."

She nods. She doesn't have much of a choice, and she hates relying on other people, but she trusts Brad. He means what he's saying. She can feel it. There's no pressure from him for anything more, even after everything that happened in the garden. She really feels safe. She hasn't felt that for a long time. And from such a very attractive man, who's standing right in front of her, half naked.

He doesn't step closer, but she's suddenly very aware of his cedarwood and musk scent. His eyes drift to her lips as he whispers, "I can still feel you."

Goose pimples rise on her skin. He's not even touching her, but her core is throbbing with need.

"It's not as strong," he says, taking in a deep breath as if gathering himself. "But I can feel you're still unsatisfied. And since you're stuck here with us, I thought maybe we can help each other. If you want." He keeps the distance between them, and the message is clear - he's not touching her, and he won't, unless she says yes.

Tenuously, she feels for the connection with Irene. It's still there, as she knew it would be, and through it she feels Brad's desire for her. It's not as urgent as it felt before his earlier release, but still sharp - almost painful - needy. For whatever reason, he needs her - not just physically.

There's pain in Brad, a palpable grief. Cassia thinks of her own childhood loss. She'd never known her father, so she understands all too well what it's like. And it doesn't seem so bad wanting comfort in another person's arms.

She's not sure how much he realizes she can feel through the connection, how much he knows he's revealing himself, but she doesn't care. He might use her for tonight, but it's from need rather than callousness. She turns towards him, leaning in to kiss him hungrily.

He returns her kiss with no less intensity, claiming her mouth with impatient abandon. But she pulls back, wary, to look him full in the face. She needs this, she realizes. To look into his eyes.

She's never been a great judge of character, and when she got together with Darren, she was drawn to something tender in him too - something vulnerable and unsure. When she got to know him better, she realized he was unsure because he was lying to her. And she kicked herself because she had always known on some level - had known it in the way he never met her eyes when they were making love. He was always holding something back, his gaze dancing away. If he were here now, his gaze would graze her open dress, exploring her body, but not her soul.

He never wanted her, not really. He always wanted what she could do for him.

Brad's eyes stay fixed on hers.

"What do you... what do you want, Brad?" she asks him.

"I want you," Brad says, eyes intense on her.

She laughs, her eyes flicking down to his erection. "Yeah, I can see that."

He grins, but he cocks his head to the side. "You're unsure?"

"No, I... I can feel you too," she says. "But more than physically..."

He flinches. "Sorry about that," he says. "Mummy issues are probably more than you signed up for." He sounds... regretful? And vulnerable.

And that clinches it. He didn't lie or hide from the truth. His grief is like a scarlet letter and he's being honest and attaching no strings.

She reaches for his face, stroking it tenderly. "Hey," she says, "We all have issues, yeah?" She lets some of her own vulnerability shine and kisses him tenderly.

He kisses her back, tentatively at first, then more deeply. Leaning in, his hands twine in her hair, and she runs her hands along the hard muscles in his shoulders. He kisses her neck and she groans gently. His hands knead her thighs, and when he parts them, she lets him.

He trails kisses down the front of her open dress, eyes on hers in question when he reaches the most intimate part of her.

His tongue flicks over her clitoris, and she throws her head back and closes her eyes in pleasure.

Across her eyelids dances an impression of Lincoln. Lincoln's eyes, Lincoln's lust, Lincoln's tongue, and the intensity in his eyes.

She imagines him palming himself and watching Brad pleasure her.

The thought of Lincoln pleasuring himself adds to the mounting pressure inside her, a rising wave that causes her eyes to fling open.

And watching her through the now wide-open doorway, is Lincoln.

She gasps, shocked, and Brad looks behind him. He grins, seeming not at all bothered. "Round two, hey brother?" he asks.

"Well, I was coming to say I got everything you need from your house, Cassia. But you were making quite a lot of noise," Lincoln says, leaning against the doorway with his arms folded. He's sporting an impressive erection pressing against the dress pants he's still wearing. His eyes flick over Cassia's gaping dress, although Brad's body is covering her more intimate parts. "Don't stop on my account."

Brad turns to look at her and raises an eyebrow. "I promised to satisfy you," he says. He leans forward to kiss her on the mouth gently, and then the ear. "And I can feel you like him watching," he whispers into her ear. "But we can ask him to leave if you like."

He pulls back and looks at her in question. It's a genuine question, and she likes it. After being disarmed by seeing

Lincoln, Cassia feels in control again. She grabs his face and kisses him hard. "So satisfy me," she says when she breaks off.

Brad meets her energy to claim her mouth with impatient abandon, then pulls her off the sink and spins her around. He presses her hands flat by the sink. In the mirror, she sees Lincoln watching with hungry eyes as Brad pulls her dress down, exposing her breasts to the air and pinning her arms to her side. He lifts the hem of her dress without ceremony and presses his cock against her entrance, his sweats in a quick pool around his ankles.

She leans over the sink to allow him easier access. Her body is already wet and ready. He pushes into her slowly, meeting her eyes in the mirror as he does so. Her breath comes in short sharp bursts, her own gaze torn between Brad and Lincoln, both watching her avidly.

Lincoln's eyes meet hers in the mirror as Brad fills her to the hilt. She moans. Her body sings at the sensation, her hands grasping at the cold ceramic while the rest of her body lights on fire. Brad's holding back - torturously. Her eyes switch to his in the mirror. She's had enough control from the West boys to last her a lifetime.

She bucks back against him, wanting more, moaning and pushing her need into the connection with Irene. She wants him to take her - hard. And she wants Lincoln to watch.

She can see it when Brad's control snaps, hear it in his sharp intake of breath. He braces a hand on her shoulder and plunges into her again, pumping furiously, his expression almost pained.

When the wave crests in an explosive orgasm, Brad swears and groans, joining her in orgasm. Her vision goes hazy as her body collapses against the sink. His arm wraps around her, his forehead resting on her shoulder. She's not sure if he's bracing himself or holding her up.

She laughs, a nervous habit, and turns to face him and connect. Or maybe say thank you for some of the best sex she's ever had.

But as she turns, she glances out the window and sees her ex, Darren, watching her with an open mouth from the bathroom window of her house.

# Chapter Eleven

## BRAD

"What is it?" Brad asks, alarmed when he feels Cassia stiffen beneath him. Then he follows her gaze out the window. He sees something moving but doesn't catch a face. He doesn't have to - Irene has already reached into Cassia's house and dragged a dangling man out the window into the night.

"Do you know who that is?" he asks, letting her up from the counter.

Lincoln has already left, out the door and into the garden, so Brad doesn't feel like he has to leave her yet.

"My ex, Darren Brently," she says tightly. He can tell it isn't a welcome visit. Anxiety is coming off her in waves, her eyes fixed on her own bedroom window, as if she wants to check what he's disturbed.

He's reminded that Cassia's unusual for a witch - she's left her coven. What little he knows about witch communities means they'll try to get her back. His mother changed her name when she left her own community and rarely ventured out of Healesville.

A protective urge surges through him. She looks small right now, vulnerable in her ripped dress. She's all alone in the world. He can understand that.

"We'll take care of it," he says, putting his hand on her shoulders.

For a second, she looks like she'll say yes. But she shakes her head. "This is my mess - you've been very..." she laughs, and looks up at him with a cheeky smirk. "Kind is not the right word. But you've been very understanding."

He frowns. She's determined to be independent - he can understand that. But she's wrong about this. That guy was out to harm her, broke into her house. But it has to be her choice. "Irene will hold him until you decide."

Her face goes blank, and he knows she's checking with Irene. Her expression clears, and she nods at him. "Thank you. And I might need those clothes after all."

"Take your time. He's not going anywhere," he says. She looks at him uncertainly. He can sense she doesn't want to face her ex smelling of sex. Good, that gives him some time with the asshole. "Seriously. Shower if you need to. We'll take care of it." He pulls his own sweats on and leaves the room.

He tests her feelings through Irene - they're distant but there. It feels a bit like spying, but then he knows she has access to as much through the connection as he does. And he doesn't mind that at all, that she knows more about him. It saves him having to share things he doesn't have words for.

She's anxious, and underneath that, she's afraid but... hopeful, mixed with tenderness. His heart leaps with hope of its own, but he clamps it down. He hadn't been thinking about the future, but maybe there's more outside Healesville than just an escape.

He wanted to see if she was feeling okay about the intruder. Oh who was he kidding? He wanted to know how she felt about him, and about Lincoln watching them. He could feel how much she enjoyed it, and he loved riding her high, but Lincoln and he had shared girls before, back in Healesville. When they were an experimental bang, and nothing more.

He was surprised at the sudden anxiety that gripped him after they'd made love. It felt right, being sheathed inside her. It felt like a place he never wanted to leave. And there's no guarantee he can keep her - he's painfully aware that there are no guarantees anyone will stick around.

For years, apart from family, his interaction with other people has been basic – fuck or fight. But he could get used to the feeling of Cassia in his arms, right when he's the most aware he could lose her. It scares and confuses him enough that he's more than ready to kick the shit out of the intruder to her house.

He doesn't get a chance before Cassia catches up to him. She kept her shower quick.

The trussed-up intruder is a pretty boy about Cassia's age in a black t-shirt and cargo pants. Irene has him tied and gagged, a few inches off the ground in front of us, but he's fighting as hard as he can. Lincoln pretends to read on a nearby garden chair, one leg crossed over the other.

Cassia's wearing Brad's sweats and t-shirt when she joins them outside. She looks cute in the oversized clothes. They completely hide her shape, but the hard nubs of her nipples are easily visible. She looks down at them and scowls, twisting the bottom of the shirt into a knot at the front to crease the fabric. It makes them less visible but reveals a strip of her brown waist.

He wants to slide his hands around her skin there and nuzzle into her neck. Instead he steps behind her and runs a hand down her back while she faces her ex.

"Irene's had a busy night," Brad remarks.

"Good for her to get some exercise," Lincoln says, putting his book down. Brad recognizes it as Crime and Punishment, Lincoln's favorite.

Brad wills Irene to release his gag. When the vines untwirl and the man speaks, Brad steps forward and punches him in the face. Darren's nose spurts blood. He looks horrified.

"Hi Darren. What were you doing in Cassia's house?"

Cassia makes a shocked sound behind him. He's not sure how she's going to take this, or whether she'll like it, but this guy is going to pay for what he's done.

Darren splutters. "You'd punch a man with his hands tied behind his back?"

"He has a point there, brother," Lincoln concedes in a drawl. He stands now but still hangs back, arms folded. Irene releases Darren's arms.

Brad punches him again. "Hi Darren. What were you doing in Cassia's house?" Darren looks at Brad with pure hatred.

Brad looks back at Lincoln with a raised eyebrow. The edge of Lincoln's mouth turns up in a slight smile.

"How did you get in, Darren?" Cassia says, voice hard. She's standing on the other side of him, far away from Lincoln. Her arms are wrapped around herself protectively. The urge to go to her wars with Brad's urge to punch Darren in the face again. "I have wards on the house that should have alerted me."

"I know, I was there when you laid them, remember? I knew you'd lay them back when I left, so I left a backdoor. Don't worry, I'm the only one who can get in," Darren says.

"Oh, I'm so relieved," Cassia says bitterly. "As long as it's just you, then. And not someone incentivized to see me fail."

"Who is this creep?" Brad asks. He looks down his nose at Darren. The pretty boy looks smug, considering the black eye emerging on his face. Brad doesn't like him. He hits him again.

"Stop," Cassia says unconvincingly. "Stop. There's no point in beating him up further. What the hell were you doing in my house, Darren?"

She's interrupted by a low booming noise, and flames erupting from the windows of her house.

Lincoln springs forward and wraps around Cassia in a flash. Brad finds himself on the other side of her, although the explosion feels contained apart from the heat from the flames. It looks like some of Cassia's protection wards are still in place.

And then Cassia's going nuts - beating against them, screaming and crying, and trying to push them off her to get to her house.

"Let go of me!" she screams, eyes full of anguish, fixated on the flames.

"You can't go over there with the mind meld," Lincoln says, as cold as ice. That's Lincoln for you - all practicality. She shoots him a look of pure venom and Brad feels sorry for him as she beats against him, but he helps hold her down.

"You asshole!" she screams at Darren. "What the hell have you done?"

Her rage, her despair, all flow through Irene, and vines wrap more tightly around Darren's arms and legs, creeping up to strangle his neck. Brad checks on Irene and can feel her intent is to make Darren afraid, maybe hurt him, but not to kill him. Right now, Cassia isn't showing as much restraint.

"Brad," Lincoln snaps. He nods his head towards the burning house and reaches out a hand for his brother.

Brad doesn't hesitate, and in the back of his mind, notices how unusual that is. He knows what Lincoln is proposing. They've dealt with fires before, even though it seems unlikely that vine mages would be the best to deal with fire. Any ordinary vine can suffocate a house so no air can get in.

Normally, they wouldn't try this with Irene - especially not after moving her so recently. Their connection to her means she feels loss when she's injured, and she hates being limited by the long regrowing period necessary after this kind of work.

But this time Irene is willing - she wants to soothe Cassia's anguish.

And more surprisingly, Lincoln is willing. Lincoln who rarely lets his emotions show, who seemed to spring from nowhere to wrap himself around Cassia when she was in danger. Later, they'd have to discuss why Lincoln was so carefully controlled around Cassia, but couldn't seem to stay away from her.

Brad takes Lincoln's hand, and they stand with legs spread, hands to the air. Nearby, Cassia goes quiet when Irene's vines shoot up towards the house.

Irene is bigger than you can see from above the ground. Paired with the mage's magic, she uproots herself from all the small spaces she's curled into, to wrap entirely around Cassia's house. Lincoln wasn't lying when they told Cassia that Irene couldn't extend into her house on her own.

It's taking a huge amount of energy and effort for the brothers to grow her so quickly that she can wrap around the house. Ignoring the searing heat, she winds herself around every window and crawls into every crack.

Darren watches the house from his restraints, eyes wide as if he can't believe what he's seeing.

Brad can feel Irene delicately crawling through Cassia's things to find the fire. She concentrates on the heat, pouring vine upon vine onto the flames to suffocate them.

Her leaves sear and become fuel, the smaller twigs turning to kindling. The smell of her burning fills the air, overpowering the existing smell of the burning house. Her root systems begin to show, ripping out of the ground around her and wrapping around Darren so the rest of Irene's vines can join the fight.

Still she pours more on through the licking flames. She's determined, he can feel it. Her loyalty to Cassia is surprisingly solid. And with their focus on the flames, Brad and Lincoln's connection is more open to each other than normal. They're similarly focused, as if it were their own house, or their own family.

That's why they keep going, pouring more of Irene's root system out of the ground, until she's barely holding on, until she's completely enveloped the house.

Then they stop. They can't move until the flames are smothered completely. Brad tries not to look at how little of Irene remains.

Sweat runs down Brad's face, and Lincoln looks haggard as the minutes tick by. Cassia's gaze never leaves the house, her face pale and drawn.

When Irene finally withdraws tired branches from the house, Brad rests his hands on his knees with a deep exhalation. There's not much of Irene left, but she's still alive.

Behind them, Cassia runs through the house to the front door.

It's Lincoln who moves first, stumbling after her. "She broke the connection with Irene. Who knows how that will effect her. And she could hurt herself in there," he mumbles, looking unhappy about it.

Brad should feel jealous, and maybe if Cassia had chosen Lincoln first he would be. But Lincoln has been different since their mother died. Distant. Obsessive. He was falling apart as much as Brad, in his own way.

Lincoln's interest in Cassia started because of what she could do for them. But now it's moved beyond that. She's melted his brother's heart. And it's hard to feel jealous about that.

"Better go after her then," Brad says with a smile.

"What does that mean?" Lincoln says, spinning. Behind Brad, Darren is almost completely cocooned in Irene. He's making soft signs of distress. The mages ignore him.

Brad grins at Lincoln knowingly. "We could have let the house burn. If it were anyone else's house, you would have. If it were anyone else, you wouldn't care if they hurt themselves running into an obviously damaged house. Cassia's got right under your skin."

"And you're so immune?" he snaps.

"Aw hell no, that woman has got her hooks in me good. That's how I can recognize the signs. It's ok brother, you're in good company." Brad pats him on the back as he walks past. "We can talk about what it means later. Now let's go get our girl."

# CHAPTER TWELVE

# CASSIA

From the outside, the house looks fine - the door is almost untouched. But when Cassia pushes against it, it swings open loosely, and she can see the marks of soot along the walls. The smell is almost unbearable, the air still thick with smoke. She leaves the door open behind her, and her heart pounds in her chest. She's not sure she's ready to see what's happened to her beautiful house. What that monster Darren has done.

She feels so stupid for assuming Darren wouldn't come back! She'd let her guard down, relaxing and enjoying herself with the boys, foolishly hoping for a future for herself free of the coven.

She steps into the kitchen, where the oven hangs open. It's bad in here - black marks lick up to the ceiling, and the counters are seared, the pots and pans askew either from Darren or Irene's passing, she's not sure. It's still so hot it's almost unbearable, so she turns away. She doesn't need to see any more there.

The stairs creak underfoot as she makes her way upstairs. She ignores the sound of the boys behind her. She's not sure she could face them right now - not sure she can face anyone. There isn't as much smoke as she was expecting, although her eyes and throat still sting in the aftermath of the fire.

Did Darren know she wasn't home? Or was he intending on starting the fire with her in the house? She shakes her head at the thought while she takes another stair, slowly edging her way up to her bedroom. Streaks of black line the wall outside her bedroom, and her stomach sinks. Darren knew how much she loved her bedroom. She stops, taking shallow breaths because of the smoke, but biting her lip to keep back the scream.

"Man, he did a good job," Brad says behind her. Lincoln follows behind, still inspecting the damage through the door to the kitchen. "Looks like he started one in the kitchen and another upstairs. That your room?" he nods up ahead.

She doesn't respond, just keeps going, each step like lead until she can swing open the bedroom door. It's a wreck. The beautiful vintage look is gone, soot streaking every surface. Her vanity is blackened, and clearly the source of the fire, with a glass of what looks like an incendiary potion smashed on its surface.

She tries to keep it together. Her shoulders cave in, and she clutches at the doorframe of the beautiful bedroom she spent so many hours redoing. The first bedroom that was solely hers, and not given to her by someone else out of charity.

All the months of worrying about whether the coven would catch up with her, and whether she could keep herself afloat out here on her own. Whether she even deserved a place as beautiful as this. It all rises to the surface. Despair sweeps over her in a dark wave, and she takes a step into the destroyed room.

The floor gives way beneath her foot. Her leg goes clean through. Her arms desperately flail as her body follows... When her wrist is grabbed and she's tugged backwards. She falls back into powerful arms which tug her back to the doorway.

She collapses into Lincoln's hold.

He locks onto her like a vice, protecting her from collapsing. He's warm and rock solid, and she knows he won't let her go. The comfort of it, contrasted to the despair of her life falling apart, is overwhelming.

She freezes.

It would be so easy to let him hold her. To soften against him - to cry and let him comfort her. To let out all the pressure she's had building up since Darren left.

But she barely knows Lincoln, and the last time she let herself relax with someone, it was Darren. The man who just blew up her house.

The thought of Darren anchors her with rage, and she pushes herself from his grip. Lincoln lets her go as she walks away, back towards the brothers' house.

She can collapse later. After revenge.

She strides through the ruin of her house, out the front door. She doesn't look any further at the wreck around her. Her mind is clear. If she focuses on Darren, she can get through this. She can take action, and then she can grieve the life he stole.

She walks straight past Olivia in her driveway. She's wearing jeans and a t-shirt and carrying a bunch of red hemlock in a floral arrangement. At another time Cassia would have found it cute. Olivia calls out, "Are you okay? What happened?" She should respond, but she can't think about anything else right now but Darren, and revenge.

All three of them follow her into the boys' house, straight through to the backyard. They follow at a respectful distance. She dimly hears introductions behind her. Then she picks up the knife Brad dropped earlier in the garden.

It's Olivia who wraps her in a bear hug this time. Cassia had forgotten how tall Olivia is, how broad. Olivia is formidable, black dreadlocks falling down her back, dark muscles bulging as she pins Cassia's arms to her side.

Darren stares at them both from where he's still wrapped in vines, eyes wide. He struggles against Irene's vines.

Cassia throws her head back to headbutt Olivia, and Olivia says, "Woah there." She picks Cassia clean off the ground and shakes her from side to side until Cassia drops the knife.

Cassia screams in frustration. It feels good, so she keeps going. When she's done, some of the fight leaves her. She sags in Olivia's arms before feeling her feet touch the ground again.

When she can think straight again, she notices Lincoln looking at Olivia suspiciously.

At that moment Darren breaks his arms free, ripping himself away from Irene's vines. He doesn't get far. Brad steps forward and punches Darren in the face. Staggering back and holding onto his nose, Darren is still bound from the waist down. Brad steps forward and grabs him by the front of his shirt.

"I'd like to know what's going on here," Olivia says, "but I get the impression I'm better off asking that guy." She nods at Darren. "He's the one responsible for the house?"

Brad nods. "Cassia's ex. She was here when it happened. I'd like some answers out of the fucker myself."

"I'll help," Olivia says.

"Are you helping as a friend to Cassia or a representative of the orcs?" Lincoln asks.

"Orcs?" Cassia asks, twisting her head around to look at Olivia, who still has her wrapped in a hug. Olivia releases her and steps back, looking sheepish.

"I guess the jig is up. How did you know?" Olivia asks Lincoln.

"You're the bodyguard of a rich and famous man who just came out as an orc, and you look almost identical as a human to your orc form," he says. "How could anyone NOT know?"

"Most humans don't notice," Olivia says.

"Most humans aren't mages," Lincoln says.

Cassia looks between them, confusion turning to frustration. "What are you talking about?"

"It's probably best if I just show you," Olivia says, and breathes in audibly. By the time she's breathed out, her skin is green, she's gained a couple of inches of height, and her muscles and shoulders are more pronounced. The clothes she was wearing still fit, but are tighter in her new form, like they were designed for this shape. "Surprise."

# Chapter Thirteen

# LINCOLN

L incoln folds his arms while Olivia does her magic trick. He watches Cassia out of the corner of his eye. She looks like she's about to faint. Of course she's not okay - her house just caught fire. But that's not his major concern.

There are a million questions he has to ask Olivia - and Darren. But right now, he's mostly concerned about Cassia's well-being. Because she can help them with the grimoire, of course. And for Brad's sake. And not because the sight of her in pain wrenches something primal deep inside him.

He can deal with that later.

Irene is weak. Darren shouldn't have been able to break her vines. And Irene has dropped her connection to Cassia on the way to the house next door. There's no telling what the break in connection could do to them both. Cassia could be seriously hurt in ways that aren't immediately obvious.

He's a fool. In trying to help save Cassia's house, he might have killed her.

"What do you want with Cassia?" Lincoln asks Olivia bluntly.

"I'm a friend, and a client," Olivia says defensively. In her orc form, the woman is huge. He believes her - she saved Cassia from herself earlier. He's glad for that. He's not sure if he could fight Olivia with Irene out of action.

But the orcs have their own problems, and he's not naive enough to believe Olivia is among magic users for no reason. Buying from them is one thing. Creating personal relationships is another.

"Why are you her friend?" he asks bluntly.

Olivia's eyes slide to the side. Cassia's face creases in hurt and she puts a hand to her forehead. How much has this woman been lied to? She steps backwards, away from Olivia, further into the garden.

"I needed some potions, and I like her. That's the truth." Olivia says it directly to Cassia before her eyes turn back to Lincoln. "And a witch was mentioned in our prophecies. The tangled witch. It's not easy to find independent witches, let alone ones whose magic could mean entanglement."

Brad shoots Lincoln a look he tries not to notice. Meanwhile, Irene's vines creep on the ground towards Cassia. Of course, Irene would want to re-establish connection. Whether that's a great idea right now is another thing. Once the connection is broken the damage is done. At this point, there's no telling what reconnection will do. Before he can say something, Cassia's head is bowed, one hand on her forehead. Her knees go first.

Brad steps towards her and calls her name as she collapses, sweeping her into his arms and away from Irene's creeping vines.

As Brad carries her into the house, Lincoln follows. Brad shoots him a smug look. Brad has always been perceptive, and he seems to have a clearer read right now about what Cassia could mean to them.

The look is because usually Lincoln doesn't stick around when things get complicated. He's never stayed for the hard things. His lovers never seemed to mind. They complained, but they always came back for more. He had thought it was despite his hot/cold routine - he got bored easily and never bothered hiding it. Eventually he realized they liked it - it kept it exciting for them. Brad never had time for games like that, and he did fine.

Lincoln was used to it, and could hardly complain. But he got tired with dealing with the constant drama, and he could tell Brad was unsatisfied with pressing drunk women up against walls.

Lincoln was surprised Cassia was interested in them both. She seemed more connected with Brad than that. But witches were more sexually liberal than the mages Brad and he grew up with.

It feels different with Cassia. Maybe because of Irene's connection. Maybe because she's beautiful.

Whatever the reason, he desperately wants her to open her eyes.

He looks at Brad. His forehead is creased in worry, his eyes fixed on Cassia's face. This is the most animated Lincoln's seen Brad in months. He hasn't been sure lately about whether Brad is going to stick around. He shakes off the undercurrent of worry about that - he promised their mother he'd look after Brad.

Instead, he focuses on the woman in Brad's arms. He wants her to feel comfortable. He wants her to like them. It's really quite embarrassing, so he shakes that thought off, too.

Brad puts her down gently in the spare room bed. It's a blank room - but homey, like the rest of the house. Lincoln sits behind her and checks her pulse - it's there, but weak. He waits with it. Her skin turns pale, her pulse weaker.

Brad comes back in. Lincoln didn't notice him leave. "Irene is retreating into herself. Darren's bonds are getting pretty weak," Brad says.

Lincoln doesn't respond. Despair rises in his chest. Irene goes dormant when she's injured - she hibernates. But she's a plant. What will Cassia's body do in response to that?

While he watches, her breathing stops. He swears and starts mouth to mouth. Brad and Olivia urgently whisper behind him, but he remains focused on his task until Cassia takes another shallow breath.

Olivia hands him a pre-opened bottle of juice.

"Try this," she says. "It's my emergency stash healing potion. If she's the tangled witch, she's linked to my people, and under our protection."

"Tell him what it is," Brad says, from the doorway.

"You're really going to make me say it, aren't you?" she says, and squirms. "It's my queen's secretions, generated during sex, usually only tasted by the king. And I can tell you he isn't crazy about me having some, but it's an incredibly powerful healing potion."

Lincoln takes the bottle, mind whirring. Irene is a magical creature, harmed by a physical act. Her link with Cassia is magical. Fluid generated through a physical act from a magical creature could work. But he hesitates. "Have you tried this with humans before?" Lincoln asks.

Olivia shakes her head. "It's a last resort," she says.

Cassia takes a shuddering gasp and stops breathing. The room stills until she takes another breath.

"Think it's time for the last resort," Brad says.

Lincoln takes the bottle from her and pours some of it between Cassia's lips. Nothing happens.

He debates pouring more in, when she coughs. Her eyes are still closed, but he encourages her to sit up, and she drinks shallowly. She spills some of it over his sheets. He doesn't care. When he's certain she's taken a sip or two, he lets her lie back. Her eyes slide back shut.

He hands the rest to Olivia. "Pour the rest on Irene. And I trust you'll take care of Darren." He looks at Brad at this last instruction. "Tonight we got an excellent taste of why our mother was in hiding for so long."

Darkness crosses Brad's expression. The grief is always there, ready to swallow him whole.

"Screw that coven," Brad says. "I want some answers." He gets up and storms out. Olivia follows.

"Olivia," Lincoln calls after her before she gets too far. She stops. "I would normally advise Brad to be prudent. But I trust the orcs will manage whatever happens out there."

Olivia looks down to where his hand clasps Cassia's before moving back up to his face. "I'll take care of it," she says, and then turns to leave.

"Also - he won't think of it - but take one of the vines from the second bedroom out to him. One of the big white pots. They'll come in handy." She cocks her head at that, but nods.

A part of Lincoln wants to go with them, but a stronger part keeps him where he is, watching Cassia's face, waiting for her to wake up.

# Chapter Fourteen

## BRAD

Brad storms out into the garden, fists ready. Darren is free of his vines, trying to climb a wall. Dead lines litter the garden.

Brad's heart aches for Irene. He can barely feel her - when he reaches for her he gets echoes of pain and exhaustion.

It's satisfying to drag Darren down and punch him repeatedly in the stomach, venting Brad's worry and rage into his fists.

"Easy, tiger," Olivia says. He turns and sees she's holding one of the vines from his room. Probably Lincoln's suggestion. It's smart. He's got to remember - he's here for answers, and if he doesn't step away from Darren now, he won't get any. He'll kill him, and get them in deep shit with a coven after them and no mage community to back them up. Besides, he's never actually killed anyone before.

He steps back and uses the rest of his rage to dig a hole with his hands in the garden.

While he's distracted Darren tries to run again. Olivia punches him in the stomach, causing him to curl up into a ball and groan. Then she picks him up by the scruff of his shirt and lifts him off the ground like he's nothing. She's seriously scary.

Brad holds his hand out to Olivia and cants his chin at the plant. She uses her other hand to pass it to him. He unpots the vine from his bedroom and puts it in the ground.

"I guess we're not playing good cop, bad cop then," Olivia says.

"I want him bleeding," Brad says, and breathes hard. "But I want answers more."

When vines from his bedroom plant curl around Darren, trussing him up and knocking him to the ground.

Brad crouches next to Darren. He wants to punch him again, as hard as Olivia just did, but he also wants results, and he's not that comfortable beating up a man who can't fight back.

Normally it's Lincoln who does the cool-headed stuff, Brad who does the punching. But tonight he has to play both roles. And it's up to him to get results.

He slaps Darren hard across the face instead. Darren looks up at him, shocked and indignant, despite a bloody lip and a growing black eye. Brad grins. It's a good compromise.

"You know, I'm a vine mage," Brad says. "People wonder at the way we control plants above ground. What people often forget is what we control underground. And at our command, you'll be dragged underground so deep nobody will ever find you." Brad causes the vines to curl a little tighter around Darren's ankles.

Darren's eyes go round with panic. Brad releases his gag. "Please... I was under orders! The coven wants her back."

Brad stands back, next to Olivia. "Does the coven burn down the house of everyone who tries to leave?"

"The... they don't like people leaving..." Darren hesitates.

"What else?" Olivia asks.

Darren shakes his head. "Nothing. Nothing more. They don't like people leaving."

"Looks like we're done here," Brad says, and the vines at Darren's ankles pull him hard, the dirt under his feet parting to allow his feet, then calves, to be swallowed.

Darren starts talking in a rush. "No wait! They don't like people leaving, but they usually let them go unless they're... valuable. Cassia's the only one who can work her mother's potion properly. We found out she was selling again. She's outselling all our love potions - it's too much competition. And her mother... her mother wouldn't share it either..."

Brad and Olivia share a look. Darren isn't a very good liar, and at the mention of Cassia's mother, Brad's heart goes up a notch. It's not a good time in his life to bring up mothers. "What about her mother, you piece of shit?" Brad demands. He instructs the vines to drag him down further until he's chest deep in dirt.

"I didn't do it! I wasn't old enough! Please, it wasn't me!..." He struggles, tears running down his face. Brad instructs the vines to drag him under the ground. The garden is silent without his pleas.

Olivia raises an eyebrow. Brad looks at her. Then he uncovers the asshole, letting the vines push him back up to the surface

Darren takes a big gasp of air, and coughs out dirt.

"I don't think the mage is playing," Olivia says.

But Darren is already speaking. "She... she wanted to run. They got the potion spell off her before she left. But it doesn't work for anyone outside her family. They knew that, so they wouldn't let her take Cassia with her..."

Brad frowns. "She said her mother died in a fire."

"No, they... that's what they told her. They wouldn't let her take Cassia. But she was supposed to leave her grimoire, too. They tried looking for her but they couldn't get to her - I heard she'd joined some mage community..."

Dots connect for Brad. Could Cassia's mother be his own adopted mother? It's possible, if Darren is telling the truth. There is a resemblance between Cassia and his mother, now that he thinks about it. They have the same dark hair, and something about the curve of her chin... It's all too much to process though, and no way to prove it right now.

Olivia's looking at him. "Is that everything you need?" she asks.

He nods. He has no idea what to do with Darren now, but fortunately, Olivia seems to have an answer.

She kneels down in the dirt by Darren's head. "Cassia is my friend, and she is now officially the witch supplier to the orcs. We have a lot of influence in this world, and we don't like people who hurt our friends. You take that message back to your coven." She stands and dusts off her knees, then stands and walks back with Brad into the house. Brad locks the back door behind him. He mentally shuts Darren away - he has to, so he's not tempted to go out there and kick Darren's head in again.

At the front door, Olivia stops, speaking quietly into the hushed house. "I suggest you keep him until morning then let him go. He shouldn't be any more trouble. We can knuckle through the details of Cassia being our witch supplier later." She doesn't mention the unthinkable - that Cassia might not wake up properly.

Brad's stomach churns, and he knows his fears must show on his face. "I'm sure she'll be okay," Olivia says. "I can tell you care about her. It's good to see her with people who care. I get the impression she's been alone for a while."

After he shuts the door on Olivia, he swings past the spare room. Lincoln is still there, worry etched on his face, holding Cassia's hand. Brad's heart stirs at the sight - at Lincoln's obvious attachment.

He's not exactly jealous - yes, he wants to be holding Cassia's hand. But he knows Lincoln - when Lincoln cares for someone, he cares unshakably. Cassia will always be protected with Lincoln by her side.

He puts his hand on his brother's shoulder. "How is she?" He asks.

Lincoln stirs as if falling asleep. "She's... unchanged," he says. He stands up and stretches. "I should retire," he says, and leaves, shooting one last look at Cassia's still face.

Brad takes his place, the chair still warm from his brother, gaze fixed on the beauty that's come into their lives and turned it upside down.

He recognized the look in Lincoln's face -worry, sorry, and a deep yearning. For the first time, he pities his brother. Brad knows Cassia likes him and trusts him. But she's not yet sure about his brother. Cassia's brought a hope Brad didn't think he would ever find, and he knows Lincoln can see it, and envies it. Brad can only hope for that kind of joy for Lincoln.

He stays holding her hand until he's woken by his own chin nodding onto his chest. She's still in the same position she was in when he was last awake. He drags himself to his own room. If she wakes up, he'll speak to her in the morning.

"Cassia?" Brad murmurs in his sleep.

In his dream, she's standing in his bedroom, her skin shining with an inner glow. His eyes spring open. His bed is covered in soft leaves. She's standing next to him, with the glow from his dream. She's cloaked in vines, flowers unfurling around her as he watches. A heady floral scent fills the air.

His door is ajar, pried open with flowing vines. He realizes he can see from the light cracking through the door from the hallway light.

"Hello Brad," she says, beaming at him.

"Cassia?" he asks again. He's very awake. Her eyes don't look right.

"Both Cassia and Irene tonight," she says. "I woke up, Brad. But there's something wrong."

"Are you okay?"

"I woke up, and I feel wonderful, but it's like I'm hungry. My body is fresh and has needs. Can you help me, Brad?"

Before he can answer, her leaves unfurl, revealing her nakedness. Her skin glistens with liquid. He sits up, ignoring the fact he's naked and hard. "Come here," he says, and she steps towards him, the vines falling away. When her body presses to his skin, he can feel how hot she is. He touches her forehead as she sits beside him on the bed.

Her gaze falls to his lips, her face slack. "I wanted to pleasure you, Brad," she says. She leans in for a kiss. His cock is rock hard pressed between their bodies, driving him crazy. "I need you."

He has no idea what's going on, but he's glad she's okay. It's no secret that witches use sex to channel power. Given that it was magical sexual fluids that brought her back from the brink, she must need sex now to recharge or something. Lincoln would probably know.

She pulls back and looks at him adoringly, eyes heavy lidded, sweat collecting on her brow. It's not Cassia's expression. But he wishes it was.

"Irene?" he asks.

"We're both here, Brad. Loving your kindness. Thank you, Brad. Cassia doesn't love you like Irene does yet, but she knows she could." His chest aches strangely at her words. It's almost too much. It feels like a gift - that possibility of love.

But it's not really Cassia. And she's sick somehow. Could she really need to be sexually satisfied? He can't fuck her in this state - not when she's not fully in control. But if she needs it...

He runs a finger between her lips and she sucks on his finger seductively, then draws back to straddle him. She doesn't use her hands - the vines around her lift her and place her back on him. She's definitely not herself. She sits in his lap, his erection pressing against her dripping sex.

She squirms, and her eyes roll back in pleasure. The heady scent of new flowers fills the air, and he realizes they're opening in the room around them, coming off the vines. "Please Brad. I need..." She looks at him seductively.

"I think maybe we should check with Lincoln about what's going on with you," he says, hating himself even while he says it.

She pouts. "Don't you want me, Brad?" Her lips curl into a mischievous smile, and he finds vines rapidly twining around his hands and ankles, wrenching his legs apart as she lifts off him, hovering in the air above him. "We can both take our pleasure," she says, and floats down to take him in her mouth.

He strains against his bonds helplessly. She smiles up at him as she laps at his cock, alternating with plunging it into her mouth.

His eyes are closed, cursing his body and hoping she's okay, when she floats above him again. "Cassia, stop, this isn't you," he says, panting. Without her mouth on him, he can think again.

"Please Brad, I need it," she pleads. "We need it to be strong again." The look in her eyes is both lustful and helpless, but he's still struggling with the logic of it when she mounts him. Her head is thrown back when he breaches her, her eyes fluttering closed, and she groans as she lowers herself slowly onto him completely. The feel of her wetness wrapping around his cock makes him arch against his bounds and curse.

It's only when she looks down, catches his eye, and smiles, that he sees her - the real Cassia - inside the creature that's both Cassia and Irene. She smiles at him beatifically as she rides him, and he says her name like a prayer.

"We're both here Brad. Thank you. We need this." Then she picks up her pace, taking her pleasure while he braces himself. Soon she's crying out, clenching around his cock so tightly it tips him over the edge with her. Stars explode in his vision in another earth-shattering orgasm. The kind only Cassia's capable of giving him.

When she's done, she collapses against him. The vines holding him uncurl, and he wraps his arms around her. She's sweaty, but her temperature feels normal again. She's boneless and satisfied against him.

Her breathing slows. He means to stay awake, to ensure she's really okay. But sleep pulls him under.

# Chapter Fifteen

# LINCOLN

Lincoln wakes with a start. He knows, instinctively, that Cassia's okay. He gets out of bed, pulls on some pants and walks to the spare room. Cassia is inside, breathing deeply, sleeping peacefully.

A heady, floral scent fills the room.

He doesn't know what it means, but he knows she's okay. He had intense erotic dreams of her - her and Brad. They weren't only sexual. He saw a connection between them he couldn't help but envy. Cassia's shown a sexual interest in Lincoln, but he can see the bond between her and Brad growing.

Then he had a strange dream where Cassia visited him, gazed at him lovingly, and kissed his forehead before retreating. He no longer thinks it was a dream. But was it Irene controlling Cassia's body? Or was Cassia involved at all? He can't dare hope.

Now it's daytime, and he's back in control.

He kisses her forehead, as she did in his dream last night, and lets himself quietly out of the room. When he reaches the kitchen, Brad's already there, with the grimoire and two cups of coffee, and of course no shirt. It doesn't annoy Lincoln this time. Brad has a crease of worry in his forehead. He cares for Cassia deeply, and Lincoln can live with that. He's happy his brother has found someone wonderful. Mostly happy, anyway.

"Tell me," Lincoln says.

"The covens don't like people leaving," Brad says. "Especially if they're valuable. Cassia was valuable. Her mother was too. Her mother wouldn't share either. She tried to run, and they told her she could go if she left Cassia behind."

"My mother died in a fire," Cassia says from the doorway of the spare room. Her voice is firm, although her arms are folded tightly, her shoulders tense. She looks normal, not possessed in the way she was last night in his dreams.

"Cassia!" Brad looks relieved. He goes to her and puts his arms around her. Lincoln looks away as she embraces him back. "I'm glad you're okay."

Within his embrace, she says it again, but uncertainly this time, with a tremble in her lip. "My mother died in a fire."

"That's what they told you," Brad says grimly.

"Is Cassia safe from the coven now?" Lincoln interrupts.

"Olivia wants to hire Cassia as the orcs' official magic supplier. If you're comfortable with it, it will get the coven off your back, and she implied it would be pretty big money," Brad says to Cassia. "In return, she might call on you to help them at some point."

Cassia shakes her head. "Of course. I could really use the money, and Olivia has been a friend."

"What about Darren?" Lincoln asks. Brad's stroking Cassia's back now. She leans into him.

"He's alive. Still in the backyard in case you had any further questions. Olivia and I also put the fear of god into him, which might come in handy if we need anything more from the coven. There are still missing pages in mum's grimoire, after all." Brad says with a grim smile.

Lincoln taps the grimoire in front of him. "Which brings me back to this. We need to identify the family of the grimoire," he says.

Cassia nods. "The page that identifies the family has been ripped out." Lincoln carries it towards her, holding the book out to her like a book stand, taking the weight of the tome. She splits off from Brad and walks towards it.

Lincoln wishes he could hold her too, but he knows they're not there yet. Not close enough. Might never be. He's happy she's awake, and near him.

She looks up at him with uncertain eyes. "So you think maybe your mother is the same as mine?..."

"Our adopted mother," Brad intervenes. She looks at him and he grins. "Don't make it weird, sis."

Lincoln rolls his eyes. "Why don't we find out," he says impatiently. "Can you identify some spells you might remember of your mother's?"

She looks at Brad as if looking for safety. Something in Lincoln's chest squeezes as Brad smiles reassuringly. But then she looks at Lincoln. It's a small trust, but he likes it. It makes him feel relaxed and tense all at the same time. He feels in his bones the dream he had of her coming to his room wasn't a dream after all. He nods his encouragement.

Cassia bites her lip, frowning, and flipping through pages. "There's the love potion but I know it's not in here. The contents page is ripped out, so I can't even tell from that."

"Would there be any other way?"

"Well - I could try a spell from the book. Witch's spells are designed to be used by family lines. That's why my mother's love potions are stronger when I make them. There are some really simple spells in here."

"Anything for healing?" Lincoln asks. "Brad keeps running into doors." Brad pulls a face at him.

She flicks a few pages and frowns. "Yes, actually. A really simple spell for cuts and bruises. Do you have any right now?"

Lincoln looks at Brad, who rolls his eyes. "I don't actually have any injuries right now, thank you very much. But for the sake of the experiment..." He grabs a knife from a kitchen drawer and slices his palm over the sink. Blood drips down his palm.

"Brad!" Cassia says, and jumps up.

"You're an idiot," Lincoln hisses.

"It's okay, my witch will heal me," Brad says, but he winces. Lincoln knows he was cutting himself for dramatic effect, but probably went too far. His blood falls in a steady stream and his face is pale.

Cassia grabs the grimoire out of Lincoln's hands and brings it to Brad at the sink. Her eyes are fixed on a page of the grimoire and she chants unintelligible words over and over, then puts the book down, cupping her hands around Brad's. She closes her eyes to concentrate.

A pink glow starts between her fingers. Brad glances at Lincoln. It's working. Cassia opens her eyes and Brad uncurls his fingers, revealing a whole and uncut hand, with only a thin white line where he'd sliced it open.

Cassia begins to cry, and Brad wraps his arms around her. Lincoln smiles and ignores the tug of envy in his heart. This is why Cassia feels right - why she's with them. Eventually, she leaves Brad's embrace and turns to hug him too.

# Chapter Sixteen

## CASSIA

"So they're like your brothers?" Olivia says in the far too crowded cafe. Someone at another table glances around. Cassia shushes her and takes a deep sip of her coffee to hide her embarrassment.

It's been three weeks since the night her house exploded, and Darren was tied up in the brothers' backyard. She didn't want to see Darren after realizing who her mother was. She was happy to know he wasn't dead, but that the brothers took care of it. It was a weird feeling, to have someone take care of things for her.

This is the first time she's had a chance to see Olivia since that night. She's been busy fulfilling the dramatic uptick in orders Olivia has put in now that Cassia is the official witch for the orcs.

"We're obviously not blood related, but that's not strange to them. Their mum - my mum - adopted them both. So yeah, it's a bit like having a family, what with my house still being out of action."

"You know we can fix that for you," Olivia offers again. "Seriously, we have a ton of orcs looking for a constructive reason to get out and about."

"I know, but the extra orders you're putting in will more than help me get back on my feet. And I like doing things myself."

"Just so you know you're not alone in this," Olivia says. "But it sounds like you're not alone right now at all." Her mouth quirks up in a half smile. "How's the sex? I knew you were with Brad, but I'm banking on both now."

Cassia feels her face going red again. She chokes, even though she hasn't taken a drink of coffee. "I haven't been very... It's complicated."

Olivia raises an eyebrow. Cassia purses her lips together. For the past two weeks, Olivia has been checking in on her. Cassia can tell that regardless of any orc prophecy, Olivia genuinely cares. It's nice to have a friend again. She may as well enjoy it.

"Well, obviously you've been keeping me busy, and the boys have been amazing helping me fulfill orders. Brad even wants to build me a website. And, of course, having my mother's grimoire is incredible. Lincoln has to chase me out of the kitchen at night so he can cook dinner. He's really an excellent cook."

"That sounds adorable. So what's the problem?" Olivia asks flatly.

"I just... well, I really like it. Brad helps Lincoln cook every night, and I lay the table. They're telling me things about my mother, and I'm teaching them about the coven. It's the closest thing I've had to family in a long time." She bites her lip. "I don't want to lose it." She frowns. "But it hasn't even been an issue, really. I mean, usually I suck at self control, but my libido's been really flat since the last time I merged with Irene."

"That really weird time?"

"Yeah - it was like I was both of us at the same time. We merged into something bigger than ourselves. And Irene - she loves the boys. She's devoted to them. So I wonder how much of my feelings for them are the remnants of that. Or maybe I feel this way because I'm stuck and don't have anywhere else to go. Or because I'm lonely and it's been so long since I've had people around. You know? I just want to give it time, so maybe it's good my libido is so flat."

"So the way you feel - it's about both of them?"

Cassia shakes her head, only realizing the truth as she does so. "I definitely feel strongly about Brad. But about

Lincoln - I don't know. Is that wrong?" she asks, with a worried frown.

Olivia shrugs. "Normal among my people. But only you can make that call. From what it sounds like, you have a big old case of the commitment phobias. Your libido might be scared into silence."

"I would consider it, but Irene's been completely dormant since that night, too. And the boys are worried. I've been looking for spells that might help in the grimoire. The love potion page is torn out, but I found a similar spell with a note that suggests trying it again to reset the connection."

"Isn't that dangerous?" Olivia asks, eyebrows raised.

"Yeah, it is," Cassia says. "And Lincoln would never let me do it. But it might be worth it."

"How much of you wanting to do this is about concern about Irene, and how much is wanting your libido back?" Olivia asks bluntly.

Cassia considers the question honestly while they both sip their drinks. She's not offended. It's something she's been considering herself. She connected with Irene and she wants her to be okay, but there's also been tension in the house about their sleeping arrangements.

Brad hasn't pushed, but she knows he's been wondering. She remembers everything she did with him that night she was merged with Irene - and she's not surprised he's interested in more.

She's enjoying getting to know them both, but she misses the spark of libido inside her too. Although it got her in trouble sometimes, it made her feel alive, and she enjoyed the connection she had with Brad in the bedroom.

Eventually, she'll want to find out what the future holds for her and Brad. And she wants to know if that spark of attraction she felt with Lincoln is still there.

"Honestly, sixty percent libido," she says to Olivia finally.

"Then screw what Lincoln thinks is safe. You should do it."

# CHAPTER SEVENTEEN

## CASSIA

C assia kneels down in the dirt, knees bare under her repaired spell-casting dress, and pours the bright pink potion into Irene's roots. She presses her hand into the wet earth. The lights are off in the house behind her, so she's only lit by the ambient light of streetlamps and nearby houses. She stands back anxiously, waiting in silence. Around her, dead vines hang listlessly. They're all that's left of Irene.

She's been wired all day, thinking of this moment. If it doesn't work, at least she tried. The brothers need never know.

It's been two months since the rejuvenation from Olivia's potion. Eventually she took Olivia up on her offer, and the orcs have done wonders with getting her house back into a good condition. They've still got a couple of rooms to do, but they're leaving it in a much better place than it was before.

In a week, she's due to move back to her own property. She'll miss the boys, she knows she will. She knows it enough to try this.

She's been planning it all week. Lincoln is out, Brad's asleep, and it's midnight - the witching hour.

The porch light goes on behind her. "What are you doing?" Lincoln asks sharply. She takes a breath before turning to him. He's wearing a cravat. She makes fun of what a ridiculous dandy he is, but she has to admit he looks good. But then, he'd look good in anything.

"Nothing you would approve of, so you should go to bed," she says, inwardly cursing. Their interaction has settled into a spiky banter they both enjoy, but that doesn't mean she enjoys upsetting him.

Brad comes out behind him. "What's going on?" He's wearing his characteristic gray sweats and no shirt.

"Ask Cassia," Lincoln says tightly.

"Is that mind meld potion?" Brad asks sharply. Her lips tighten but she says nothing. "Shit, Cassia."

"It's the only way to heal Irene," she says. "I know you're both still worried about her. There was a clue in the grimoire."

"And you didn't think to consult the vine mages who might help this ill-considered endeavor?"

"Would you have let me do it?" she asks tartly.

"Hell no," Brad says.

"Absolutely not," Lincoln says simultaneously.

"Well then, I didn't tell you." Her hands tingle, and she looks down at them, then at the surrounding vines. "I think I feel something."

Lincoln frowns, and she knows he's reaching out to Irene. "I can't feel anything yet."

He's sexy when he frowns, she realizes, but mostly because he cares so much. Lincoln would do anything for her - it's an idea she's had to get used to. It's taken two months to really let it sink in, to let him care for her.

*Lincoln is still lonely.*

The thought cuts through unexpectedly. She looks at the brothers and smiles. "I can hear her!" she says. The vines around her shift, and a tendril of a vine curls around her ankle.

"So can we," Brad says, a brilliant smile lighting up his face. He's as gorgeous as he's ever been, but his sexy edge is tempered now - she knows how big his heart is, how nerdy he can be when he's teaching her about using the website, and how goofy his sense of humor is. *All that and a lot of hard body*, she thinks, and realizes the thought is her own.

The libido that she's been missing for two months comes back in a surge of realization, looking at these two men in her life. A flush rises to her face and suddenly she can't look straight at them. "Er, well, I'm glad you're feeling better, Irene," she says. The vine curls further up her calf.

Lincoln steps forward and kneels on the ground, touching one of Irene's roots. "We haven't heard from her in weeks. Now our connection is back, our magic will revive her quickly." Under his hands, the root shifts, sinking further into the earth.

Around them, the limp leaves stir as if moved by an invisible wind. They tremble and stretch, growing thicker. Green pushes through to the surface of leaves and vines. In moments, Irene is looking healthier. Nothing like she was before, but definitely improved.

"Oh, this is amazing," Cassia says, beaming at him. "I was so worried!"

"Are you feeling like yourself?" Brad asks, concern in his voice. She knows he's thinking of that night two months ago, in his bedroom.

"Yes, I... I can feel her, but I'm not merged like I was. I don't think I'll lose control again."

Lincoln steps towards her. "Thank you," he says. "I appreciate you did this for Irene, and for us." His eyes are intent on her.

Her heart leaps in her chest. Having him so close is firing her libido unexpectedly. She can't seem to tear her eyes away from him, can't help but notice his gaze falling to her lips.

Brad comes up beside them and wraps his arms around her from behind. "Thank you. You're the best. And the band is back together. But I can't believe you're moving out! You belong with us," Brad says. "Can't you feel it?"

She smiles and leans back against him. He's right - she can feel it in the arms around her, and the time she's spent with them. The feedback from the way they feel about her is clear through the connection. The trust, the love. She feels safe with them - has felt safe for the past two months, without her pesky libido getting in the way. But now she both feels safe, and an increasingly urgent desire to wiggle back into Brad's naked chest and sigh.

Through their connection, she can feel his need respond to hers. Brad kisses her neck and runs his hands over her shoulders. She closes her eyes and tilts her head to the side.

Images of Brad pleasuring her when she was tied up in Irene, and feedback of her pleasure, resonates through the connection with Irene. The intensity of it almost makes her knees collapse.

*She likes it.*

"Yes, she does," Lincoln says wryly. She gasps, breaking the kiss off abruptly. She had forgotten Lincoln was there, standing in front of her, watching them, and feeling all the lust flowing between them.

That's when Irene yanks her up and backwards sharply, yanking her from Brad's embrace.

She was so wrapped up in her lust she didn't notice the vines had twined around her waist, her wrists and ankles. They now have her completely caught and gagged, hands pinned behind her back.

"Woah!" she tries to yell through the gag. Irene puts her back down gently until her feet are on the ground, facing away from the brothers, who've cleared a space.

The vines wrap around her shoulders, supporting her. The vine around her neck pushes down until she's bent over, her underwear on full display. A vision of Lincoln and Brad spanking her vibrates through the connection, plucked straight from her head.

"Oh!" It's Brad - shock and lust competing in his voice.

"It's amazing what you can pick up through Irene when we're all connected like this," Lincoln says mildly. "And Cassia has quite the imagination."

She can't help the searing lust she knows is raging through her connection with Irene. This image is straight from her most secret desires. Through that same connection, she feels Brad's eagerness, and she's relieved.

She also feels Lincoln's raging libido. He's so controlled she hadn't seen it for the past two months, but it's like an inferno, almost overwhelming in its need, and something like reverence. He wants her. And he's been waiting a long time.

"I think it's quite fitting to punish her, since she put herself at risk tonight without telling us," Lincoln continues.

"Completely fitting," Brad says. She can feel his eyes on her as vines twine through her underwear and drag them down. The vines hold her fast as she's exposed, Irene ignoring her struggles. She whimpers against the gag, her mind a fog of lust.

She feels the ragged edge of Lincoln's control fraying as he looks at her naked and increasingly wet pussy.

The gag at her mouth loosens, and she feels a push from Irene.

"Did you have something to say, Cassia?" Lincoln asks, voice teasing. She doesn't remember him being able to read this much of her, but she can tell he's plucking the fantasies straight out of her head. So, she shouldn't feel any shame at all, but her face still burns when she says "Please... I'd like to be punished..."

There's a pause from behind her that feels like it lasts forever.

"Would you like to help me discipline our pretty witch, brother?" Brad says, voice thick.

"Oh yes," Lincoln says. She feels them arrange themselves behind her, one on either side. Her skin is electric with anticipation, sensitive to even the heat of their skin radiating onto her.

The first spank comes sharp and hard, and she jerks against her bonds. Equally as shocking as the pain is the zing of pleasure to her core.

The second is on the other cheek, heavier but somehow not as sharp - that's Brad. They take turns, rotating the area their slaps land so the pain never grows too intense in one spot. Soon the entire surface of her ass is burning, and juices drip freely down her inner thighs.

"Such a pretty witch," Lincoln whispers in her ear. "I would love to taste you." His hot tongue flicks into her ear. A helpless sound of desire emits from her, and a part of her wants it - so badly. But another part is unsure, with Brad watching, how much of this she'll regret in the morning.

Whether this will change the connection she's found with the brothers - or jeopardize what she has with Brad.

"But I believe Cassia has been punished enough. Over to you, brother," Lincoln announces. She feels him retreating, but soon sees him before her - he's grabbed a chair. And he watches while she feels Brad's whole tongue plunge into her.

Lincoln's still fully dressed, his cravat high at his neck, while she loses control. He has a tight smile on his face, but his eyes are feverish as he watches her face.

Brad's hands are braced against her thighs, holding her spread open while he pushes his face further into her, stubble adding a painful sensation that tips her over the edge.

She cries out and arches against the vines in a wave of euphoria. Her body squeezes around his tongue, an intense orgasm clutching her body in an almost painful cramp. All the while, Lincoln watches, erection straining against his pants.

As the waves of pleasure leave her body, the vines slowly unravel, leaving only one curling vine wrapped around her ankle.

Her legs give way, but Brad sweeps her up in his arms. "I've got you babe," he says. She wraps her arms around his neck and leans her head into his chest, eyes sliding shut in a blissful haze.

Brad carries her inside. She's aware of Lincoln following behind them. He stops at the door to his bedroom. With the mind meld so strong, she knows they'll feel him release into his palm later. He'll be alone, while Brad and her have the comfort of each other. It feels cruel. Wrong.

"Wait," she calls out, twisting her head to see him. Lincoln stops halfway through his bedroom door, turning to her. Brad puts her down, and she walks to Lincoln. "I just want..." She starts, reaching a hand out towards him, but she stops. Her instincts have led her here, but she hadn't thought this far ahead. What happens tonight could change everything, and she's not sure she's ready for it. Her chin furrows, and she feels foolish.

Lincoln takes her hand and steps towards her. He touches a knuckle to her chin, leans down and kisses her gently on the lips. The kiss is sweet and reassuring, a thanks for her compassion. She closes her eyes, leaning into it. Her confusion eases. Lincoln cares about her, and would never hurt her.

But then he pulls back, and naked desire shimmers in his eyes. She feels it then, beneath the surface. A dark promise that makes her breath catch. He doesn't want her compassion. But when she's sure, he'll be ready. "Get some sleep, witch," he says, and turns back to his room, closing the door.

She turns back to Brad, self-conscious, but he reaches out a hand to her, a smile quirking his lips. She smiles back and takes his hand, knowing it's okay, and follows him to her spare room. She sinks into the bed and Brad shuts off the light and scooches in beside her. The connection through Irene is still strong, and she can feel Lincoln in the other room, Irene through the vine at her ankle, and Brad beside her. His arms wrap around her, and she sinks into the smell and warmth of him, enjoying the new sensation of feeling completely at home.

# THE WITCH'S TANGLE

L.A. MONTEIRO

CHAOS ELF PUBLISHING

# CHAPTER ONE

# CASSIA

I'm in my newly refurbished vintage-look kitchen, stirring a bubbling potion on the stove at midnight. The liquid in it is almost clear, with potion ingredients swirling within. My mother's grimoire is open on the table beside me, fitting right into the dark wood decor.

I'm stirring with my left hand because my right arm is in a cast.

Brad's arms are wrapped around me from behind. He's not wearing a shirt, as usual, and his cedarwood and musk scent fills my world. It's my favorite smell, and in his arms is my favorite place to be. My gaze runs along the tribal tattoos that extend down his right arm.

He kisses my ear and one of his hands dips low, pulling up my plain black spell-casting dress and tucking a hand into my underwear.

At our feet, the sentient vine Irene rustles with irritation, and Brad chuckles. Irene found sex fascinating when we first connected. Now she mostly finds it boring - all squishy parts and hormones.

Meanwhile, I find Brad incredibly distracting. But sexual energy is an amplifier of magic, and I'm hoping his presence will give me a boost.

He laughed when I first told him my plan but was quickly on board.

I gasp as he slides his fingers along my sensitive core. My hand on the wooden spoon clenches.

"Have I told you how much I love helping?" he murmurs into my ear while his fingers distract me.

This is more than a frustrating experiment. None of my mother's spells have worked for me. I've always been good with spellcasting, and I've been training since I was ten, like all witches in my coven. My family spells should be easier than any other, but right now my skills are failing me.

These aren't just spells to me - they're my past, my family, my connection to my mother.

It could be because my mother's spells are trickier than the test spells the coven used for learning magic, but I could weave her love spell with ease. Her other spells should be just as easy, including this unbinding spell.

It's upsetting that her spells won't work for me, but more than that, I'm worried about my connection to Irene. Well, maybe not worried exactly... not worried enough to tell Brad.

Guilt sinks my stomach.

As far as Brad is concerned, the mind meld faded a month ago. He doesn't know I can still hear her. He doesn't know about my fainting spells. The last one happened while I was carrying a box of moisturizer from one room to another and resulted in my broken right arm.

The concern in his eyes when I woke up almost made me confess... but something held me back.

If Brad knows, he'll worry. He'll tell Lincoln, and they'll try to separate us. Irene doesn't want that. And after years of being a strong independent woman, I don't want that either. I'm not ready to be forcibly removed from my only friend, as tragic as that is.

I can handle it on my own. Probably. But this unbinding potion will help smooth out the wrinkles of doubt I have about the connection.

Fortunately, it's only Brad I have to worry about. Lincoln's been avoiding me since the night both boys pleasured me in the garden. I don't know what his problem is.

*You want each other, and you're not ready for the complication.* I push Irene's intrusive thought aside. It's harder to lie to yourself when you have a permanent guest in your head.

I try to clear my mind, putting the spoon down to rest in the cauldron. My gaze finds the incantation for the spell in the grimoire.

As I start chanting, Brad kisses along my neck. My breath huffs out in a shudder. I can't feel him mentally like I could a few weeks ago, but I feel his erection pressing into me, and he's as hard as a rock.

My left hand shakes as I hold it above the cauldron.

Irene huffs in amusement. I'm careful not to react to it, but I shift my mind to her, to step back from my body while I chant.

The concoction in the cauldron shines with an unnatural light, breaking me out of my reverie. Hope flutters in my chest, and I chant louder. This is further than I've gotten before.

Brad reaches a hand up and pinches one of my nipples. My eyes flutter shut with pleasure. I slam my good hand down on the counter, bringing back my focus. The lust is feeding the spell so we can't stop, despite the torment. I keep chanting while he kneads my breasts.

"You're so wet, baby," he says into my ear, and plunges a finger inside me. My chant falters.

The bubbling cauldron instantly goes black. It turns from the clarity of a mountain lake to a thick, murky pitch.

I curse.

Brad pulls his hands out of my dress. "Too much?"

"No, it's not you," I say, turning around to wind my good arm around his neck, my cast pressed between us. When I pull back, I take him in.

His gaze is fixed on mine, and it still makes me catch my breath. He's still as gorgeous as he was when I first spied on him from my bathroom window. But now he's all mine. And sometimes when he looks at me, I feel like he loves me. But he hasn't said it yet.

The idea that he might say it makes my heart ache and my mind scramble. Men have told me they love me before, and it's never lasted.

*Humans are so temporary,* Irene says with disdain in my head. Brad doesn't hear her. My gaze slides to the side, away from him. I'm not sure when she learned to block him out when she chose to, but she's been doing it more and more.

"It was a long shot, anyway. I haven't tried that in years," I say out loud.

"You've tried sex during magic before?" Brad asks, eyebrows raised. His mouth quirks into a kissable cheeky smile.

"You're imagining the witch version of a pillow fight right now, aren't you?" I ask.

He gives a panty-melting smirk instead of answering, and my heart flutters.

"Would it interfere with the fantasy if I told you the other witch's name was Michael?" I ask.

"It would modify the fantasy," he says, and kisses my neck. I close my eyes and sink into him. When we first met, his touch was electric, but now it's something more - warm, familiar, safe, building a heat inside me I never want to end.

*It's dangerous.* It's not Irene this time, but my own thoughts warning me. My own history, coming back to haunt me.

*Brad isn't dangerous,* Irene points out.

Memories of past hurts rise up, and I talk out loud to distract myself from my silent conversation with Irene, and the guilt that pits in my stomach at lying to Brad about her.

"We were young - fifteen - and Michael was obsessed with amplifying magic. Mostly because he had very little talent, to be honest. Maybe that's why I'm thinking of him now. I was the talented one, even though I had no family pedigree. His family was one of the ones who fostered me, and they were impressed with my magic. They kept me longer than most families did."

He pulls back from my neck, and I meet his gaze. I don't talk about my old days in the coven very much. But Brad's a good listener. And as I think about that time, old hurts rise to the surface.

"Did he take it hard when you left?"

"He was already gone when I left. He was sent away. After we…" I falter, embarrassed. I never could control my libido very well.

Brad doesn't seem to mind. He chuckles.

"I was considered a bad influence, and his parents were worried I'd corrupt their wonderful son. So, he was sent to another coven, away from my womanly wiles. And my talent didn't stop them from passing me on to the next foster family. Last I heard, he was married in another coven." My story ends with a bitter note in my voice. Michael's family was the closest thing I had to a home.

Until now. I'm not sure if that thought is Irene or me. My stomach churns. Sexual relationships aren't built to last. I've learned that from hard experience. I learned that the first time with Michael. I'm not sure if I loved him, but he was probably my only friend, and I ruined it.

Brad presses his forehead to mine. "You were young. We all make mistakes. And they were all idiots for not seeing you for what you are," he says.

His voice is so tender I can't help tears from welling. Guilt adds to the churning confusion in my gut. "What am I? A witch who can't work her own grimoire?"

He cocks his head to the side, waiting for me to get it out. I wipe at my tears. "Sorry, I... I'm just frustrated. These spells should work better for me than anyone else. It's my mother's grimoire. And I can DO binding spells." Many of the spells in the book are about connection, binding and unbinding creatures together. And none of them work.

I lean my forehead against Brad's chest, and he strokes my hair. "It's not in your nature to give up." I shake my head into his chest. He's right - I fight, even when it's foolish.

I sigh. At my feet, Irene rustles and gathers more closely around me, twining around my ankles. I pull back from Brad's comfort. "I'm sure the missing pages have the key. We need to get them back."

I've been keen to go back to the coven myself and demand the pages, but Brad thinks the coven will fight me. So that means finding another way.

The boys have been asking around - using whatever sources they have to help us get into the coven, or for someone to sneak the pages out. So far, they've turned up nothing.

"It's taking so long!" I say, pushing off him, my frustration mounting.

Irene soothes me silently, and the tension in my shoulders eases. And it's not just Irene I can feel anymore. I'm getting impressions of all the plants around me - a sense of their health, the feel of the earth pressing around roots.

Witches shouldn't be able to sense things like that without a potion or spell. It's kind of freaking me out.

I shake off the thought. I swear I'll tell Brad everything - as soon as I get this spell working. Then he doesn't have to worry.

"The day doesn't have to be a complete loss," Brad says, as he leans down and kisses me deeply. When he pulls back, I'm breathless, leaning into him again.

He slips his hands under my dress, cupping my ass and lifting me up so my legs wrap around his waist. He's strong enough that it feels easy to wrap my good arm around his neck and hold on. The vines at my ankles slip away. He carries me up the stairs to the bedroom.

He throws me backwards onto the bed and tugs my underwear down, throwing them in the corner while he lowers his head to my sex. Before he gets there, he pauses and looks into my eyes. "We should have dinner with Lincoln sometime."

My heart leaps in my chest. It's a dirty trick, bringing up Lincoln with me when I'm worked up and willing to agree to anything. But Brad only knows half of what I'm feeling and thinking right now.

For a second I don't respond, and I know he can feel the conflict pulsing through me. "It's okay to want things, Cassia," he says. Then he grins. "God knows, I could use a hand keeping you satisfied sometimes."

My guilt soars at that. Brad does keep me satisfied - he's the perfect boyfriend. But my crazy libido can't help wanting Lincoln. Then he bends his head to my sex, and I stop thinking at all.

# CHAPTER TWO
# LINCOLN

I point the remote at the TV and press the button. The glow from the screen lights up the dark hotel room. Behind me, Vera is tied spread-eagled to the king-sized bed, face down, wearing nothing but the vines that tie her to the bed. That's where I left her when she fell asleep earlier.

The vines extend from the lovingly tended potted plants that sit beside the bed, and on every spare surface of the boutique hotel room. The attached bathroom is similarly full.

I'm wearing a crisp white shirt and dress pants. My shoes are still on. We both like it when I stay in control while she loses hers. My cravat sits in a crumpled ball beside me, however, in concession to the night's exertions.

On TV, a news presenter stands in front of the Orc Rights Association. "...Tom Johnson has publicly condemned the actions of his people."

The image switches to a press conference, where Tom speaks. He's handsome, in his mid 30s, and looks every bit human. A pretty brunette stands behind him.

"It is unsafe to mate with an orc. If you genuinely suspect you have orc blood, please contact the Orc Rights Association. And to my people - please be patient," he says, with a nod at the woman behind him.

The on-screen caption reads 'Tom Johnson - Orc King'.

"That was Tom Johnson speaking out about the increasing number of women injured after attempting to have sex with orcs. The situation escalated quickly after Summer King, soon to be Summer Johnson, revealed herself last year as a mystic - a part orc woman. The question now is, how long until this situation reaches breaking point?" The news presenter's tone is ominous.

A scoff sounds from the darkness behind me. Vera's cynical voice comes from the bed. "If those women can't stay away from the promise of giant orc cock, they deserve what they get."

I turn off the TV, stand and walk to her. I flick on the light by the bed. A black cocktail dress is a crumpled mess on the floor. She's right at the edge of the bed, her head facing the TV, where I wanted her.

Her flawless pale skin shines in the dim overhead down-light, her dark hair a messy tangle. Her athletic body is magnificent. Only a bit of red on her ass-cheeks and the flogger lying on the bed beside her give away our earlier activities. That and the moisture shining between her legs.

"I see you're awake," I say, picking the flogger up. "And compassionate as ever."

Another scoff. "Those orcs are a danger to us all. It won't be long before the humans get curious about other magic."

I should have brought a gag. It's strange to hear Vera use the term 'us'. Vera is a mage, and technically I am too, but my half normal blood makes me and my brother outsiders. It's why we moved away from Healesville - why we moved away from all my kind.

Vera is the only one I've seen in months, and I try to keep the information flow between us one-way. Mages don't like outsiders. They stick to their own.

Thinking of Cassia makes my heart hurt. Her sweetness is a sharp contrast to the bitterness of Vera's tongue.

Cassia's part of the reason I've been seeing Vera more lately. Vera's husband has useful trade ties to the witches and might have a lead on where to find her mother's grimoire. Her mother who was also our adopted mother.

I land a couple of sharp whacks on Vera's ass. She gasps. "Don't mark me!"

"I never do," I remind her. Her husband wouldn't like that. To wipe the thought of that from my mind, I dip a finger into her still soaking sex while I smatter blows to her back and shoulders. She squirms for me, and I keep going until she's gasping. This is the other reason I see Vera - to blow off some steam.

Face down like this, her dark hair spilling over the bed, I can almost imagine she's someone else. The thought fuels me on.

Later, when her hair is up tightly in a bun and her dress is back on, I'm watching more coverage of the orc situation on the couch when she leans over to give me a cold, closed-mouthed kiss. When her lips leave mine, my eyes return to the TV. My stomach is tight, my chest cold.

The sheets are a crumpled mess behind me and covered with both our fluids. It feels dirty, shameful, hollow.

Maybe I always felt like this after our sex. Vera and I have been lovers for a long time. But it's been worse lately. It's been worse since I met Cassia.

Vera stands still next to me, arms folded. "You don't have to be an ass about it, Lincoln," she says. "I was going to let you know Anthony is away again next Friday."

"Go back to your husband, Vera," I say, not bothering to look up from the TV.

I'm glad when she storms out.

We have a good time, Vera and I. Her tastes align very well with mine. And we do things I could never imagine doing with someone I care about. Things I couldn't imagine a girl like Cassia would want, despite the bondage and spanking that happened two months ago in our garden.

That little taste of darkness was enough to make me want more - so much more. But Cassia was still making her mind up about me, and I wasn't ready to unleash myself on her yet.

So seven weeks ago, I turned to Vera, while Cassia had Brad to keep her company. Getting the missing pages of Cassia's grimoire back, and finding out more about our mother, was just an excuse.

Vera read through my ruse - she was always good at sensing weakness. I might take the lead once we're in the bedroom, but she's the real predator. She'd brought some new toys and booked this room. And then she kept calling. She has an uncanny knack for knowing when Cassia and Brad are fucking particularly loudly. I assume it's because mages are known for their intuition. When she asks about my home life, I give her the barest crumbs.

Since that first time, I've found out almost nothing about the coven that's useful, and I've found it hard to say no when Vera calls.

Meanwhile, Cassia's grown closer to Brad, while her connection with Irene is fading at a natural rate. But Irene has been distant sometimes, and so has Cassia. When she broke her arm two weeks ago, she said she fell. But I think it might be more.

Unfortunately, I haven't been able to watch her closely. She's been avoiding me. The lust I felt from her initially is still there, but there's something holding her back. It's not Brad - he has a romantic notion that connecting her to both of us will make us all stronger. Cassia seems unsure.

I wonder if maybe it's fear. I'm not warm like Brad, I don't wear my heart on my sleeve. I won't give her anything she asks for. And in the bedroom I might give her things she doesn't ask for, however she might crave them.

I shut the TV off. I'm not watching it, anyway. But I don't move. Instead, I sit in the darkness, not yet ready to go home. Brad and Cassia are in love, whether they've said it yet or not. So where does that leave me?

# CHAPTER THREE

## BRAD

I watch Cassia snore, fast asleep, legs spread. She fell asleep straight after her orgasm, while my tongue was still inside her. It would be funny if it weren't worrying.

She's been exhausted lately, sleeping more often and working all hours, trying to keep up with new potion orders from the orcs, the love potion business she already had, and finding a solution for her mother's spells.

And then there's her broken arm. She swears she tripped, but I'm not so sure. And sometimes I swear I can still hear Irene. But she hasn't said anything.

I know she's scared, of what's going on between us. We fuck constantly, but when it comes to talking about feelings, she shies away. Without the magical connection linking us, I can't tell what she's thinking. Maybe that's a good thing. We're still new, and I can tell she has doubts - especially about Lincoln.

But I don't have doubts. I know we're right for each other, and I'm making it my mission to wipe all her doubts away.

I let myself out of the room, shutting the door behind me carefully and making my way back downstairs. The place looks a lot better than it did when I first met Cassia. The orcs helped rebuild it after the fire, and she did all the renovations she wanted to.

The front room is still full of boxes. That much hasn't changed - half of Cassia's house is overrun by her business.

Since I set up a website, and Lincoln's put his mind to some of the strategy, business has been booming. She's selling less product with a higher profit margin and edging her old coven out of the market.

They deserve it, after lying to her for years and treating her like shit.

I let myself out and make my way to my place next door. It looks the same as it did six months ago - two cute vintage Californian bungalows, Cassia's with a second storey addition. But now there are vines trailing over the fence in between the gardens and in through Cassia's windows, crawling all over the side of her house.

My Harley is sitting in my driveway, but Lincoln's car is missing. When I get to my room, I call him. He's usually done with Vera by now.

"What?" he answers abruptly.

"You get anything from Vera?" I ask.

"Nothing," he says. And then a pause, and I know what he's going to ask next. "How is she?"

"Well, she fell asleep while I was going down on her, so I'd say tired."

"Or maybe she was just bored," he throws back, but there's no heat in it. I can tell Lincoln is as jealous as hell. It would be fun if I didn't see his misery, and Cassia's angst about it. Our connection through Irene has faded in recent months, but I know them both well enough. I've told them in ten different ways, I don't mind their connection, but they won't listen to me.

Watching them dance around each other for the past two months, sniping and then shutting each other out, has not been fun. Cassia started avoiding coming to our house at all.

"How many hours is she sleeping, did you say?" Lincoln asks.

"About twelve hours," I confirm. "But she's not weaker. Her love potions are still working. She's still carting boxes around for orders. She's just tired."

"Okay. We should keep an eye on her."

"You can't watch her when you've been avoiding each other."

There's a moment's pause while the statement hangs in the air. And then he hangs up.

Olivia is sitting at a booth in the bar, chatting with the cute female bartender. It's quiet inside, with only a few other patrons dotted around. She stands out like a sore thumb, even in her human form.

She's tall for a woman, and her muscles pop under her sweatshirt. Her skin is darker than most of the people in the bar. But mostly, the thing that stands out is the way she looks totally at ease, and yet alert at the same time - as if she could take on anyone who comes at her.

I have no doubt she's clocked everyone in this room and could tell you how much of a threat they are. She could also tell you what every hot girl in the room looks like and what they're wearing. It's no wonder we're friends.

She's also a night owl, like myself, which is why she texted me back after midnight for a quick drink.

I grin as I approach, and she smiles back, natural troublemakers recognizing each other. We clasp hands and hit each other on the back in greeting, and I scooch into the booth across from her.

"For you," I say, and pull a small packet from my jeans and slide it to her along the table. It's a healing salve Cass prepares for Olivia's brother. Something I don't need to know anything more about related to orc mating.

Olivia nods and gives her thanks. She's been practically glowing lately, and I suspect a new lady, but she's surprisingly discreet about whoever her latest conquest is. I think that means it's serious - I don't kiss and tell with Cass, so I understand. I'm happy for her.

"I've got something you might find interesting too," she says.

My heart beats a little faster. I've asked Olivia to do some research into the covens. Her brother runs a technology empire, and they have a lot of money behind them. That kind of money can open doors. Despite that, we've had next to no leads so far. The witches stick to their own.

"Cassia's coven - Fairbridge," Olivia says. I nod a yes. Fairbridge is the name of the town the coven calls home. "They've been seen talking to orcs."

I raise an eyebrow. Witches and orcs aren't known for getting along. In fact, according to Cassia, the witches and mages are aligned with believing the orcs are dangerous to our people's privacy and safety.

"The friendly kind?"

"The kind of orcs who want to overthrow my brother as leader. So no, not friendly. We don't know why they're meeting, but we've been monitoring the situation. I've also got word that most of the coven council are out tomorrow night at the full moon at around 6pm, meeting with some orcs on neutral ground. If Cassia is going to go hunting for her missing grimoire pages, tomorrow is a good night for it. All the coven elders will be away."

"Thanks Olivia," I say, while my stomach churns. There's no way I want Cass going back to her old coven after they tried to burn her house down, especially not with a broken arm. But she knows the most likely places to find the pages. If I try to go on my own, I'll blow it and ruin our chances of going back again.

The orcs are another huge factor. She's wrapped up in their world in a way we don't understand, and if her old coven is involved with them, there's bound to be trouble.

I'm torn. Lincoln would be cautious, but that's not my style. I prefer to go in guns blazing, and I take what I want, or I lose. But that won't work this time, with Cassia's safety at risk.

"What are you going to do?" Olivia asks, sharp gaze on my carefully neutral expression.

"No fucking idea," I say, honestly.

An hour later, I pull into Cassia's driveway on my motorbike and see Lincoln's study light on, and his shiny new silver Mercedes in the driveway. In Healesville, we didn't bother having cars. We didn't go many places, and it was tacky to advertise how successful our business was.

Over the past two months, Lincoln has been enjoying the money we make selling witch weed to humans. Fancy clothes, the car, and regular hotel visits with Vera. I don't think it's making him as happy as he was hoping for.

When I knock on his open study door, he's sunk into his laptop. He's dressed as impeccably as always, but otherwise looks like shit. Now isn't the time to call him on his lifestyle choices.

"I've got news," I say. He closes his laptop. "Cassia's old coven is meeting with the orcs. The bad kind. Olivia doesn't know what they're up to, but she knows the coven will be nearly deserted tomorrow night."

"I'd prefer to stay out of orc business, especially with everything on the news right now," he points out.

I nod grimly. I agree. Plus, Cassia's got a broken arm, and she's been tired lately. "We don't know the place well enough to go in without her."

"Do you think she'll want to take the chance anyway?" he asks.

I nod. "She's really upset her mother's spells aren't working."

"Guess that decides it then," he says. He opens his laptop again. "We don't tell her. I support your decision. Get some sleep."

It's typical Lincoln phrasing - dismissive and somehow deciding the situation himself.

But I don't disagree. I don't feel good about it, but Cassia's not in the right place to go to the coven tomorrow, and she's too headstrong to stay home if I tell her. I feel shitty for lying to her, but maybe I can do something good to make up for it - whether she'll thank me for it or not.

"I'll need a distraction or she'll know something's up," I say. "We should have dinner here."

He stops typing but doesn't look up for a moment. Instead of responding, he just nods.

# CHAPTER FOUR

# CASSIA

Brad is a terrible liar. He's definitely hiding something. I watch him as he stands next to his brother with a bottle of wine in his hand. He's getting glasses while Lincoln cooks pasta on an enormous stone frying pan that probably cost a fortune, but he hasn't sat down next to me yet.

Lincoln is wearing a silk shirt open at the neck, a concession to the casual dinner, and Brad is wearing a black t-shirt and jeans. I'm wearing tight black jeans, some slip-on black flats and a cowl neck black top that sits low enough to be flattering without being too revealing. It took me an embarrassingly long time to decide what to wear.

The boys' kitchen should look like mine, but it doesn't. Where I got cabinetry and coloring that brought out the vintage look of my kitchen, theirs is more modern. Shiny new chrome appliances have replaced the herbs in white pots that used to line the counter. The sun is setting, leaking golden light in through the kitchen window.

Irene winds around the edges of the room, a few vines trailing from the edges to twine at my feet.

The boys are arguing about how much they should charge for shipping to a new coven they're supplying witch weed to. The argument has a well-worn feel to it, like it's been going for days and will keep going until Brad wears Lincoln down into a compromise.

A few weeks ago, I loved this comfortable sense of family. But the line of Lincoln's body is tense and permanently turned away from me. He's gotten worse around me - it's like he can barely stand being in the same room.

The feeling is mutual.

I would have canceled, but Brad was quieter than usual this morning, too, so I thought he was upset about me falling asleep with his head between my legs.

He took off for the rest of the day, mumbling something about errands. After he left, I took a two-hour nap. I've been careful not to mention how much I've been sleeping.

I meet Lincoln's eye, and he slides out of the eye contact, cool as a cucumber. It's hard to tell if he's keeping something from me. I don't know much about Lincoln these days.

Brad said Lincoln's been seeing an ex-girlfriend more. He looks tired, like he hasn't been sleeping enough. My mind shies away from how he's been spending his evening hours instead.

"Irene, extending to the table is a tripping hazard," Lincoln says, and I feel him push at her will, compelling her to move. She ignores him.

Lincoln's mouth presses into a tight line. My stomach roils uneasily. Lincoln is perceptive, and while Brad hasn't picked up on my connection to Irene, Lincoln might. I give her a mental push, and she slides away from me gracefully, into the corners of the room. When she's moved, Lincoln returns to stirring the pasta.

"The covens need the cash..." Brad says, breaking the silence and clearly trying to change the subject.

"So how was Olivia?" I interrupt. Brad looks at me blankly for a second. "I saw the package I left for her was gone, so I figured you must have seen her last night?"

He turns away from me to open the wine bottle he's been waving around, to pour it into three glasses.

"Good," he says, not looking at me.

When he puts the glass in front of me, his gaze shifts away restlessly. Olivia told him something he doesn't want me to know. That much is obvious. Now just to sniff out what.

"There haven't been any more prophecies?" I ask while he hands a glass of wine to Lincoln.

"What? It's not enough to be the fabled savior who will unite the divided orcish people?" Lincoln asks dryly, before sipping from his glass.

He's hit a sore spot and I think he knows it. The orcs have helped me a lot because of their belief that I'm special to them. I haven't done anything yet to prove it, and sometimes it makes me feel guilty, and worried I'm not what they think I am.

"She didn't ask for it, Lincoln," Brad points out.

"No, but she benefits from it. And all that orcish generosity is going to have its pay day at some point," Lincoln says darkly. "And you don't know what it is they're going to ask you to do."

"They're not like that," I snap. He's buying into my own fears. What will I have to do to save the orcs?

"Olivia had no more prophecies," Brad says, annoyed. "And you two need to get a room already."

His statement would normally embarrass me, but Lincoln has me riled up, and I know Brad is hiding something. "Did she have any information about getting into the coven?" I ask directly. Brad glances at Lincoln.

They both know something, and they won't tell me. *Of all the...*

Brad's been asking me for weeks about the layout of the coven so he can go in himself.

"You can't go to the coven without me," I say.

"We won't," Lincoln says dismissively, continuing to stir the pasta and sip from his drink with one hand. He doesn't even look at me. Brad shrugs at me, looking helpless, and very guilty.

"Then she did say something," I say, frustration rising. "Does she have a contact? Does she know where the pages are? Does she know a good time for us to break in?"

Brad's face tells me it's the last guess I've got right, and he can see it on my face. "You wouldn't make it now anyway," he says.

"And it's a terrible idea." Lincoln stops stirring, drops the spoon, and turns and faces me. "You've been weak and you have a broken arm. You can't go to the coven like this. There'll be another opportunity to go."

"So it's NOW? Was this dinner a distraction?" I look at Brad indignantly. There's guilt written all over his face, and I hate it.

"It was 6pm. Olivia said your coven had a meeting with some orcs," he admits. "That means they're planning something. We're better off monitoring rather than jumping in."

It's 6:15 now. The coven is a 45 minute drive away. I probably wouldn't make it now. Brad has ruined my chance of getting my mother's coven pages back. My stomach is heavy with dread. What does this mean - that he would lie to me like this? How could he do this to me - to us?

"Brad cares about you. And he doesn't want you to do something stupid," Lincoln says. His icy tone is clipped, his irritation rising. He's not the only one. He's the last person I want to hear from right now. There's no way Brad would have lied to me without Lincoln's approval.

"Brad cares about me - what's your excuse? Or are you just a controlling ass?"

"Maybe I'm the only person who understands you need to hear no sometimes." He's not shouting, but his face is red. And he's not the only one.

"Ugh!" I throw my one good hand out, and Irene wraps around both the boy's feet, up their bodies, up to their waists, pinning their arms to their side.

I've never seen Lincoln look so shocked. I can feel him try to get Irene to release him, and also feel his hold on her slide off. "She doesn't have to listen to you anymore, Lincoln. Neither of us do."

And then I walk out.

# CHAPTER FIVE

## CASSIA

I take Lincoln's car, and I drive it carelessly, pushing the speed limit all the way to the coven before my rage subsides.

*Stupid boys, always so controlling,* Irene says. My head is clearer now the coven is in sight, and I realize what I've done. After weeks of hiding my connection to Irene, using her to tie them up tonight let the boys know I've been lying to them. Guilt eats at me, and I try to press my foot on the brake. Irene is preventing me.

A spark of alarm thrills through me, even while another part of me accepts this as normal. Of course Irene could control part of my body - she's already part of my mind.

"Enough, Irene," I say, and give her a mental push.

She gives me back control of the brake, but says, *Time to stop.*

The Welcome to Fairbridge sign is faded from the sun, with old lettering, and brings back a flood of memories. I flipped the bird at it when I left this town and vowed never to come back.

I pull over before I pass the sign. My hands grip the steering wheel, the smell of new car and leather helping calm me.

I'm on my own, with zero planning.

*We take what's ours*, Irene says. Yeah. Very helpful. I shush her. Plants can lack nuance sometimes.

Fairbridge isn't just a town - it's its own world. A small, provincial town with no actual power in the real world, but had a huge amount of sway over my life for over twenty years. Witches are not like orcs - Olivia's people are embroiled in the human business world. The witches stay hidden and stand apart.

This town would look normal to any regular person - any normie. There are no security gates. But there are security spells - notification spells about anyone who passes the sign I'm parked in front of.

Even if most of the witches are out, the notification spells will still work. Fortunately, neutralizing the notifications was one of the first spells a rebellious teenage witch learned how to master. It's a few words and a few hand signs, which aren't too affected by my broken arm.

As I mutter the well-memorized words and make the motions, my mind whirrs.

Hiding the car will be hard. This kind of wealth stands out. But if Olivia's right, most of the town should be gone, and the few left behind won't be watching the roads. They'll rely on the notification spells.

I've considered where they might keep my mother's pages. There's a small high street, with a town hall and a library attached. Upstairs in the library are offices, and the more delicate coven texts are kept there under lock and key. My mother's pages are likely to be there, because the coven council would see the pages as belonging to them.

That's the mindset of the coven. Pure arrogance. They think they've done nothing wrong - that my mother's grimoire belongs to them. That I belong to them. I finish my chanting with that angry thought fueling me on.

My hands grip the steering wheel, and I start the car again. I drive up the main road for a few blocks, completely exposed. I don't know how dangerous the coven really is, but my mother was scared enough to never leave the mage community she fled to. The last interaction I had with them was my ex, Darren, trying to burn down my house on their behalf.

Irene stirs angrily at the thought of Darren, and I shush her again.

I think of this as I veer off to a side street, coming up towards the back of the library. I drive straight to the parking lot, which is when I notice that something is wrong. The parking lot is full.

The library building is still and dark, but the town hall next to it is lit up like a large event is going on.

My heart pounds in my chest - this is not what I was expecting. I keep driving, smoothly taking off into a quiet side street.

I stop the car and consider my options. I could go home.

*Or you could go in,* Irene suggests. I know she's just a plant in my head, but she makes me feel less scared, and less alone. Maybe it isn't such a crazy idea.

The town isn't empty. But they're busy - the parking lot was full, and there were the sounds of a crowd coming from the town hall. But the library was dark, and there's no back door to the town hall.

It's a risk, but I've come all this way. It's the closest I've come to getting my grimoire since I lost it. And the boys might not have suggested holding off if they knew how strange my connection with Irene was.

The least I can do is check the library door and know what to bring for next time.

When I get out, I notice the air smells like it always did - fresh, with hints of baked bread and cooking in the air.

The coven enjoys modern conveniences when it suits them but prefers to make most things in the town. It would be quaint if it weren't also claustrophobic. They believe the only things that matter are the town and its people.

I rub my arms as I walk to the library. It's not cold - it's memories pressing in.

The witch community was small, and their old ways were slowly dying. They saw it as the duty of the next generation to make sure we survived. They demanded loyalty.

Instinctively, I reach out with my new senses for comfort. I need a reminder that although the town might be the same, I'm not the girl who left here years ago. I reach out to feel other plants nearby.

It's a strange sensation. I haven't reached out quite like this before. I feel the roots of old trees pulsing with life beneath the pavement under my feet. It's comforting - like I'm connected to everything around me.

When I reach the library back door, I'm heartened by the noisy sounds next door. It should raise my sense of alarm, but I know this town, and when there's a gathering, everyone attends. There are no rear windows in the old building. If the door is unlocked, I might get away with finding the pages tonight with no interruption.

I check the door. Hecate must be smiling on errant witches tonight. It's unlocked. Inside it's dark and smells like dusty pages - a familiar smell. I was a studious child, and I spent a lot of time in here avoiding my peers.

Light and the sounds of chatter filter in from the town hall next door, getting louder as I make my way to the wooden staircase which is closer to the town hall. But there are no windows on this floor. The stairway creaks loudly in the darkness, but I feel safe that the sounds from next door will mask it as I make my way quickly to the second storey.

My breathing is coming quick and fast now, excitement warring with fear. I could do this. I could make it and never have to come here again.

On the landing, there's a window with a direct view of the town hall stage. I mean to walk straight past, heading to the archive room. But instead, I stop and stare. Two orcs are standing on stage next to members of the council. Laughing and smiling. The same witches, who condemned and feared orcs for potentially revealing the existence of witches to the world.

Nobody can see me from where I'm standing, shrouded in darkness in the library, on a second storey looking down on this strange sight.

One orc is huge, with an arrogant expression on his face, and a missing hand. The other is wearing a pair of spectacles that look too small on his large features. He has a more gentle expression, and stands slightly behind the other, like a servant. A council elder - Michael's father, Adam Thompson - steps up to the microphone and hushes the crowd. His hair is peppered white now, a change in only the two years since I last saw him.

I thought my heart was hardened against all the foster families who gave me up, but it still hurts, to see him.

The crowd is all the people I knew, people I grew up with, but I can't count any of them friends. They all have each other - friends and family, loyalty to the coven. I haven't stayed in touch with a single one of them.

I mean to turn away. But I find my eyes glued to the stage when the arrogant orc steps up to the mic and speaks.

"I'm so glad our people can work together with this common goal," he says. His voice matches him - gruff, arrogant, and powerful. "We will be forever grateful."

"And your support also, in returning our people to their rightful place in history, will forever be appreciated," Adam says.

Suddenly I feel foolish. Whatever I want from my mother's grimoire, it pales compared to whatever's going on in that room next door. Brad and Lincoln were right - I shouldn't have come here tonight.

As I stand there, staring at the orc, I swear, he looks up and catches my eye. He looks right at me, and my heart pounds so hard I think it'll leap out of my chest. In the worst timing in the world, my knees go weak, and blackness creeps around the edges of my vision as I crumble to the ground.

# Chapter Six

## BRAD

I deserve everything Irene is throwing at us, and more.

For the past hour, Lincoln has had his eyes closed, trying to use our magic to get Irene to let us loose. Mostly I've just raged impotently against the vines that are holding us.

My phone is in my back pocket and has rung out twice. Only a few people have my number, but I figure if it's Cass calling, Irene would let me go to pick the phone up.

I have plenty of time with my thoughts.

I should have told Cassia about the situation and reasoned with her instead of lying. But maybe she could have told me she was still connected with Irene. What kind of screwed up relationship am I in right now?

I was so afraid of losing her I tried to be someone I'm not - someone cautious, somehow secretive. And maybe she was freaked out, too. This explains why she's been so determined to get the unbinding spell to work.

I swear if I get her back, we are going to have a long conversation. And I'll lock Lincoln and her in a room and get them to sort their shit out.

Abruptly, suddenly, Irene releases us. We both collapse onto the ground at the speed of release, and I see Lincoln wince at the waves of alarm coming from Irene.

Something's wrong. Cassia's in trouble. Lincoln and I exchange a look, and I check my phone. There's a couple of missed calls from Olivia and a text.

> The situation has changed, don't move tonight - Olivia

I grab a kitchen knife before I head to the door. Lincoln follows me as I make my way to my bike, phone to my ear as I call Olivia to find out what's going on.

I know he'll be coming with me. Cassia needs us. And it's time I did things my way.

---

The town is dark and quiet on the outskirts, but we can see from afar the lights in the more densely packed center.

Lincoln taps my arm and tries to stop me a few blocks away. I ignore him and let my motorbike rumble up two blocks from the center of town.

Olivia told us the town would be full of both witches and orcs tonight, and Lincoln and I aren't prepared for a full-blown fight with only the two of us.

Our first and only plan is to find Cassia and get her out of here. Fortunately, Lincoln, being anally retentive, has a way to track his new car on his phone.

We race through the empty suburban streets, and quickly find the Mercedes. Cassia left the keys in the ignition. Lincoln pockets them and locks the car.

"Where to now?" he asks. He's letting me take the lead.

"Open to suggestions. We know she's here and in trouble."

He shakes his head. "You should have chained her to the bed," he says. It's intended to rile me, but I can hear the storm of emotion behind his stony expression.

"I'll tell you what - when we get her out of here, we can both chain her to the bed," I say.

He doesn't meet my eyes. "We should have told her the truth," he says flatly.

"Guilt later," I snap. "Plan first. Or I just blow shit up."

His eyebrows go up. "You know, that's not a bad idea."

Cassia has talked enough about the town that I know there's a library where we might find her grimoire. The center of town is most likely where the event is tonight.

So we find a hardware store, supermarket or petrol station the right distance away, and create a distraction.

We slink in the shadows around a small strip of shops, and I notice there aren't any boutiques - only food stores, candles, gifts and herbal supplies. It's like stepping into another century.

The houses are neat but dated and in need of repairs. The town doesn't let modern tradespeople into the place often.

The witches don't keep up with technology, relying heavily on their witchcraft. It's a strange way of life that doesn't help with them blending in. It's one reason mages look down on them. The other reason is that they have no inherent magic - they have to use spells and potions. It's accepted their magic isn't as strong as mages. But in the rare altercations between our kinds, that difference disappears.

Something moves in the shadows, and we slip further back. A man slips out of the side window of a house.

I signal quietly to Lincoln. The man kisses a young girl through the window before she shuts the window with a giggle. She's young - in her late teens.

The man peers into the darkness, obviously not wanting to be seen. It's only then I realize it's Darren, with a smug look on his face that makes me want to punch him. He makes his way back on the street and doesn't notice me until I step out from behind a nearby bush.

"Remember me?" I ask, a kitchen knife in my hand. "This is almost nostalgic."

His eyes widen with fear, and he takes a step back and notices Lincoln standing behind him.

"Where is Cassia, Darren?" Lincoln asks, as he grabs Darren's arms and twists one behind him.

"I don't know! Isn't she with you?"

"Try again, Darren," I say. My magic connects with the shrubs growing in nearby gardens. We could capture Darren and make him talk, but time is short. Fortunately, he remembers us well enough to know to be afraid. It's pure luck he's the one we ran into. "I don't know why you bother playing this game, Darren. You know how it ends."

But he's on his home turf, and he's defiant. "If she's come back, let her go. She belongs here. She's one of us. The children of witches always come back."

He gasps as my knife draws blood from his throat. "Let's assume she isn't still here of her own volition."

"Okay! Okay!" He gibbers, reliable old Darren. "If she is here and she's caught against her will, she would be taken to the archiving room. We don't have a prison, and that's the only lockable public room."

"Where is the rest of the town?" Lincoln asks.

"At the meeting with the orcs. At the town hall."

"Why aren't you there?"

"Lydia's parents think she's too young for me," he explains.

I catch Lincoln's eye over Darren's shoulder. "I just love learning new things about you, Darren. You never disappoint," I say. "Now show us where your house is."

<hr />

We leave Darren tied up in his front yard by his trees, far enough away from the fire so he won't die, but close enough that he can watch the fire we started in the kitchen. I don't mention the fire I started in the driveway under an unsurprisingly expensive new car.

We're almost at the library when his car explodes. Lincoln and I cloak ourselves in a nearby bush while townsfolk rush past. The explosion sounds impressive.

When we reach the library, the town hall next to it is abandoned. Olivia warned us they had moved the event with the orcs to the coven.

The back door of the library is ajar already, and we make our way upstairs, hurrying in the darkness.

I feel Lincoln working his magic with me, twining our will around the shrubbery outside the window, causing it to extend and crawl around the building, ready to break in if we need it.

When I get to the top of the stairs, there's only one room with a light on, with two burly witch thugs with mean expressions guarding it.

Fortunately, a second-storey window is open a crack, so we don't have to break any glass when vines pour in and truss the first man up. The second man breaks free, and I'm almost glad when he comes at me.

I haven't had a good fight in a long time. He knocks my knife aside and swings a fast right hook that nearly catches me, but I duck and lunge at his waist, pulling him down to the ground. He's a big man, and he rolls well, pinning me down and landing some punches that make my head ring before a vine comes up behind to strangle him, dragging him away from me.

His thrashing breaks a glass window, and I hear shouts from outside. That's not good.

"Gotten rusty?" Lincoln asks wryly, hands held up with fingers spread as he controls the plants.

"Just getting started," I say. And it feels like I could fight all night.

But first, I burst through the door. Inside it looks like another library, lined with dusty, brown-covered books.

A surge of triumph sings through me when I see Cassia. It's quickly twisted into a sinking stone of dread when I see her in the arms of another man.

# Chapter Seven

## CASSIA

I'm woken by a soft shake on my shoulder. I smile, thinking it's Brad.

"Just a few more minutes," I say, and roll over. But the surface I'm lying on isn't my own soft bed. It smells musty, with a hardness under the soft surface. It's carpet.

My eyes spring open. A man my age is smiling at me. He looks familiar, but I take a few moments to place him. "Michael?" It's the same face, but older.

He smiles, and there are crinkles in the corners of his eyes. It's the same, overly confident, lopsided smile I remember, and the same round cheeks and intelligent eyes.

My heart does a silly little leap of happiness, and I frown. My heart is a traitor. I don't know this man, and the boy I remember left me.

"Hello Cassia." He has the same soft way of speaking as he always did. My heart pounds that little bit faster. He was the only person who made the coven bearable when I was young, and I can't help but be happy to see him.

"What are you doing here?" I sit up onto my elbows, and he puts out a hand to help me up off the floor.

"I came back. It didn't work out, in Halwood," he says, as I stand.

When he pulls me up, I end up close to him, and he meets my gaze. For a moment, we stay still, and the years slip away. We're teenagers again. It's completely disarming.

"What have you done to yourself?" he asks. He waves a hand over my broken arm and whispers some words. My cast glows blue. I don't complain. It will only take a moment for another witch to heal me - it's a sad state of affairs that it's taken me so long to find someone to do it.

While he's chanting, I study his face.

Michael and I were attracted to each other in the way of young people who were thrown together when our hormones were out of control. It was me who suggested trying to amplify our magic using sexual energy. It was me who broke us.

I wasn't expecting him to declare his intention to marry me. Apparently, neither were his parents.

They didn't wait for my answer. I was a nobody and Michael came from a good family. He would have given me a good life. As his wife, I would have a place in the coven.

They never understood their quiet son, or his ambitions to do more than coast on his family name despite his lack of magic. So they sent him away, and they moved me on to my next foster home.

After that I didn't get close to anyone for a long time. But fantasising about Michael returning to the coven got me through some dark times.

And now he's back. He stops chanting. Inside my cast, my arm feels healed.

He smiles. "I'm sure I look different, after all this time," he says. His eyes are a bit sad. I wonder what he's been through in all these years.

I smile back. "Not so different."

"I think we've both changed. You're..." he searches my eyes as if looking for something. It makes me feel uncomfortably exposed. The only person who looks me in the eyes is Brad, and even that's new.

Michael's gaze is direct, almost hungry. Glittering with the intelligence and ambition I remember. My pulse picks up a notch.

"You've evolved, I think." It's a strange term, and for a moment I wonder if he's seen my connection with Irene.

I dismiss the idea quickly. This is what happens when you have secrets - you're always worried about being exposed.

"I should never have let you go," he says. "Forgive me?" I can't answer, and I'm relieved when he releases me from his intense stare and puts his arms around me, pulling me in close.

It feels... strange. Comforting. It's not sexual, unlike with Brad. Having Michael here reminds me of years of loneliness, and our friendship - the one bright spark in all the years. He was the only lover who cared enough for me to hold me like this. Something bright bursts in my chest - some old grief, and I feel like crying.

Irene sounds a distant alarm in the back of my mind. She doesn't have any sweet memories of Michael. But she remembers I woke up on the floor in this room.

Before I can take a step back, Brad and Lincoln burst in.

Michael and I jump back from our embrace. Brad is brandishing a kitchen knife.

The shock on Brad's face turns my stomach. The cold mask that falls over Lincoln's face is worse.

"Sorry to interrupt," Lincoln says wryly. "We thought you might need some help. Or not?"

"No, of course! I... Michael and I are old friends. We were... reuniting." I sound as guilty as hell, but I step towards Brad. The initial shock on his face has faded to neutral but wary, mostly aimed at Michael. I take Brad's hand and he pulls me towards him.

Two men I recognize from the coven crowd into the doorway, panting. Michael holds out a hand to them. "These men are my guests," he says. "And so is Cassia. There's no need for violence." To my surprise, he speaks with a calm authority, and the men, both much bigger than him, immediately back down. "Please shut the door. I'll take it from here," Michael says. We all wait in silence while the burly men shut the door with them on the outside.

"So, we're free to leave?" Lincoln asks, an eyebrow raised.

I shoot a look at Michael. He was hugging me, but I've barely had time to process why I'm here, and how I got here, let alone the complex feelings about seeing him again.

"Of course. The covens don't keep prisoners," Michael says. His words chill me. They may not keep prisoners outright, but they had trapped my mother and me with circumstance, and when we tried to leave, there were consequences. The bland lie reminds me of the coven elders, and I remember I have no idea how I got into this room. "I wasn't sure why Cassia was here, but we found her passed out in the hallway."

He speaks calmly, which is impressive given the way Brad is looking at him like he could throw a punch at any moment. The Michael I knew wasn't much of a fighter. But this isn't the Michael I knew. Who knows how life in another coven had changed him?

"Convenient that she passed out," Lincoln says suspiciously. I understand why he's suspicious. But I have a broken arm to prove that I can pass out all on my own.

I avoid Lincoln's gaze as I interject. "No, I... it's been happening lately," I say.

"Aren't you full of surprises?" Lincoln asks. His eyes are ice cold.

"But it's probably time to go home," I say, smiling weakly at Brad. I know I've got some explaining to do when I get home.

"Of course! But I hear you're looking for your mother's missing grimoire pages. I'd be happy to give them to you next time you visit - I'm on the council now," Michael says.

"Or you give them to us now," Brad says, an evil gleam in his eye. He lets my hand go and tosses his knife in the air between his hands.

"I can tell you where they are, but it won't do you any good," Michael says, and gestures behind him at a bookshelf. "Behind that false bookshelf is a safe. It takes three of the coven council to open it. Those pages are among our most prized possessions. Apart from our people, of course," he smiles at me, and Brad takes my hand again.

"That must be why she left," Lincoln says.

"Things are different now. She has a friend on the council. Cassia has a place in the coven, and a position, if she accepts it. Hecate knows this community has been challenging in the past, but we understand our own in a way you mages never can. How we think, what we need. We know how to support each other through all of life's unexpected changes. I think Cassia gets that. There's more than one reason to come back."

Brad and Lincoln shoot me looks, but my gaze is fixed on Michael. He's being vague, but he's referring to changes. I wonder how much he knows about my connection with Irene. And how much he can help. We were friends once.

Brad retorts. "She doesn't want it."

At the same time, I ask, "What reasons?"

"Reasons I'd love to discuss further in private. If you should choose to return, at a better time." It's a polite offer from the person I trust most in the covens.

Meanwhile, Lincoln asks, "What is your coven's involvement with the orcs?"

"We're helping fellow magical creatures," Michael says. "We provide spells that allow orcs to shrink parts of their anatomy to human size, to impregnate human women."

"And what do you witches get out of this?" Lincoln asks.

Michael smiles tightly. "The satisfaction of doing good for others." It's an obvious lie, and he clearly doesn't care that we know it.

"Well, it's been a swell visit, but it's time we were going home," I say, and squeeze Brad's hand.

"Of course," Michael says. "I'll make sure nobody bothers you when you leave. But Cassia - I hope to see you soon." He hands me a card with his name and number on it. I don't look at the boys when I let Brad's hand go temporarily and take it.

# CHAPTER EIGHT

# LINCOLN

I like routine. Routine makes everything feel normal - mundane. That's why I'm getting ready to see Vera the night after our coven adventure, cravat high on my neck.

Cassia stumbles into me when I'm getting a glass of water in the kitchen. I'm not surprised to see her. We all agreed to stick together after getting back from the coven last night. Cassia and Brad needed to talk, and none of us trust the witches. That's also part of why I need to get out.

I'm also not surprised to see Irene twined around both her ankles, up her wrists, in her hair. She's wearing one of her plain black dresses, but mostly she's wearing a cloak of Irene, and her cast is gone. She's frowning and looks like she's been crying. "About last night..."

"You don't have to explain to me," I cut her off. "I'm assuming you've explained to Brad." It comes out bitter, and I stop talking.

"Of course, you don't care at all. You have Vera, right? Brad told me about her. The woman with a husband, who uses you for pleasure and doesn't care about you at all. I assume that's who you're going to see tonight?" Her face is flushed with anger.

"Careful, Cassia, you sound like a jealous lover. Wouldn't want Brad to hear." I step towards her, getting into her space intentionally. I don't know why I do it - I wouldn't have before last night. But it hurt seeing her with Michael. And it feels like I have nothing to lose.

For a moment our gazes lock, and neither of us looks away.

"Brad cares about you as much as I do," she says. And there's something in her eyes now, and her voice, that makes me stop. This isn't a game I want to play. That there's no way I can win.

"Brad thinks you two need to get your shit together," Brad says, coming into the kitchen. To my surprise, he's wearing a shirt.

Cassia storms off into Brad's room.

Brad stays. "She's right," he says. "Vera's bad news. Always was. She can't be trusted."

He's right, and I know it. But she's what I deserve. "She gives me the release I need," I say, and walk towards the door. Need itches under my skin.

As I walk past him, he grabs my arm. "I'm worried about losing Cass," his eyes drift towards his bedroom. "And I think you can help me keep her."

"I'm not getting involved in your relationship," I say stiffly.

"It's yours too. And she's been lying to us both. And... she was tempted by him," he says. I wouldn't see his fear if I didn't know him so well.

"Have you asked her about it?"

He looks away, and for a moment I glimpse the raw pain in his eyes. "I don't think she knows what she feels. She grew up wanting acceptance from her people. But she just hasn't seen what more she could have. You can help me give her that."

"She's barely looked at me for two months," I point out. "This isn't all my decision."

"We have to show her. Like we did in the garden."

When we punished her. The memory stirs something deep within me - it's more than lust. It's almost like a need. But it's a need I can't indulge.

His mouth curls up at one edge, but it's more a grimace than a smile. "We can make her want to stay."

"You're crazy," I say.

He shrugs helplessly and runs a hand through his hair. I've never seen him so miserable. "Crazy in love." The word twists my heart. I hurt for him, and for her, and for myself. But I can't help him.

I walk out the door.

---

I'm back in the same hotel room, waiting for Vera. I'm calmer now, drinking a glass of scotch from the minibar, comfortable in the temperature-controlled room. Nothing outside this room exists, and nothing inside this room matters.

I brought a spiked metal wheel with me, and it's sitting on the bedside table, along with our customary flogger. The wheel is sharp enough to pierce the skin if I press hard enough. Today I brought some of the healing salve Cassia provides the orcs, which means I can draw blood if I choose. Vera comes harder when I draw blood. It's not something I have a taste for.

I'm hoping Vera's flesh giving way under the spikes will distract me from the memory of Cassia in the arms of another man. When I saw her with him, I saw red. It was a reminder that she's not mine - that she'll never be mine.

I know Brad and she are having very serious conversations. But me? I'm fine. Maybe they'll break up. I have nothing to lose.

There's a knock on the door. Vera. I put my scotch down and go to answer it, pushing the day, the week, and the rest of my life aside.

It's Cassia who greets me.

# CHAPTER NINE

## CASSIA

Lincoln does not look pleased to see me. "What do you want?" he asks flatly. I'm reminded of our first meeting, on my doorstep so many months ago. He's stony, arrogant, and gorgeous. This time I'm more prepared for his chilly reception.

If I must say so, I look great. I cleaned up my puffy eyes with a little enchanted face cream, loaded on the eyeliner, and left my thick curls free. I'm wearing a black knee-length trench-coat and heels.

He's wearing a cravat and suit the color of dried blood. The color makes me wonder what he has planned for this evening, and I swallow. But I'm ready for this. I'm more than ready - my skin is tingling with anticipation.

I barely clocked his outfit when I saw him in the kitchen earlier. But that was before another argument with Brad, who wouldn't believe me when I told him Michael meant nothing to me, and I wasn't tempted by returning to a life at the coven.

It's my fault - I know it is. I won't throw out the card Michael gave me. I can't. Brad seems to think it's because I don't know what I want. And part of that is because I'm resisting Lincoln. In Brad's mind, they're a team, and their future is together. All our futures are together. When I reject Lincoln, despite my own desires, Brad thinks I'm rejecting him.

And he's seen me hesitant and uncertain about Lincoln for weeks now. He thinks I won't accept who I am. The words stung - they felt true. The orcs think I'm some great savior, and Brad looks at me sometimes like he can't believe I'm real. But I'm just me - flawed, imperfect me.

Or I was me. My connection with Irene is scaring me. I tried to explain that to Brad, but he can't get over the lies I told him. He doesn't believe that my connection with Irene, and the offer of my mother's missing grimoire pages, are the only reasons I'm tempted by Michael's offer.

I need to show him how much I want a life with him. I need to show him I'm not running away from him, or from Lincoln.

So I went back to my house and did some thinking. Then I got dressed and came here.

I didn't tell Brad. Despite knowing this will help us, I have no idea how tonight will go. I wanted this decision to be my own, with no pressure.

I saw Vera in the lobby. I could tell who she was from her looks and her attitude. For a moment, when I saw her, rage overtook me. Vera was pretty, but cruel and vain - I could see it in the turn of her head, and Brad had told me as much. I let Irene take a hold of my body to tell Vera to fuck off.

Yes, it was scary letting Irene take hold. But it was also liberating. Irene is more comfortable with violence than I am.

Whatever Vera saw in my face scared her. But she still sneered at me, and said, "Enjoy. He'll come back to me. He always does."

"Not if I can help it. Lincoln deserves more," Irene said out of my mouth. I couldn't agree more.

And now he's right in front of me, looking dangerous.

I steel my spine and answer him. "I took off last night. And lied to you."

"None of that explains why you're here."

"Doesn't it?" I arch an eyebrow and push past him into the room. He lets me. My heart pounds in my chest. I'm in. I turn to face him, and undo my trench coat, letting it fall to the floor. The cool air hits my skin.

Underneath, I'm wearing lingerie that leaves little to the imagination. It's green and translucent with gold vines threaded through it, a bra, g-string and garter belt that attaches to straps around my thighs rather than stockings. I bought it last week and hadn't had a chance to wear it until now.

"I'm here to be punished." The words come out huskier than I intended. I don't know what I'm in for tonight, but I know I need to be braver than I've been before now.

Brad was right - I've been running. Running from Lincoln, running from Brad. Seeing Michael reminded me how long I was alone before I met the boys, and how many guards I've built up. I need to rip some of those down. I think Lincoln can help me do that.

He pauses and takes me in. The door behind him is still open - he's holding the handle. For a second, he stares, and I can feel the gears ticking in his head while I hold my breath. He could still throw me out, humiliated. And behind him, anyone could see me standing here in this.

There are voices in the hallway - a couple heading to their hotel room. Any second now, they could walk past and see me here. Lincoln is still staring.

As he lets it swing shut, the couple walks past. I let out my breath as he says, "Get on the bed. Face up."

I do as he orders, and vines crawl in from the ajar hotel window, and extend from the potted plants near the bed. They jerk me into a spreadeagled position. The bindings are firm, but not painful.

It takes me back to two months ago, when I knew I wanted Lincoln, and I wanted Brad, and Irene wanted us all to be together. How did things get so complicated in such a short span of time? *Take what you want and be together*, Irene says in my mind. Like it's that simple.

Suddenly my plan tonight feels far too simple, and far too complex. Would Brad really want me here, when we're on unsteady ground? The idea of being with Lincoln to fix things with Brad seems like a ridiculous idea. Have I let Irene influence me too much? My stomach churns with confusion. But there's no turning back now.

The room smells like fresh linen - sanitized, clean. The only sound is the hum of traffic on the streets below. We're only one floor off the ground, so I can still feel the shrubs outside and the vines crawling up the side of the building. I see why Lincoln uses this place for his bedroom games. In here, anything is possible.

When I'm secured, he stands back and picks up his phone.

"Hello?" Brad answers. My heart stops. I hold my breath. Of course Lincoln would call him. Will he see it as another lie that I didn't tell him I was coming here tonight?

"Hello. Are you aware Cassia is here with me?" Lincoln's tone is amused.

There is a pause from the other line.

My heart starts up again, pounding so hard it hurts. Will he think I'm running from him, and not trying to fix things? I feel sick, and I curse Irene internally. I was so upset tonight, so desperate to try anything, I must have been more susceptible to her influence.

"No," Brad says. He doesn't sound upset. He sounds... intrigued. Almost amused.

"She's here to be punished. I thought you should take part."

I pull at my arms and make a noise of protest, even as the breath leaves my body with relief. My relationship is intact.

All I have to worry about now is being tied to a bed by Lincoln. My heart pounds for a different reason and my mouth goes dry.

Can I really do this in front of Brad? Brad who loves me? I want him to believe the best of me, but will he, after this?

This isn't like it was two months ago. This isn't light play. This is Lincoln and I working out what's going on between us. This is opening a door I might not be able to close.

What if Brad sees something in me he doesn't like? Tonight could equally break us. But after last night, we already feel broken. I've been lying to them both for weeks.

Resignation sinks in my gut. Lincoln's right - Brad deserves to see this. Whatever happens next affects all of us.

"You object?" Lincoln raises his eyebrows at me. I shake my head mutely. "Good. Consider this humiliation part of your punishment. Tonight you will call both Brad and I sir, and do everything we ask of you. Do you understand?"

He presses a button on the screen and turns it around, pulling a side table over to the foot of the bed, so Brad can see me, and I can see him.

Brad licks his lips when he sees me tied to the bed. He adjusts the phone at his end, and I see he's in his room, lying on the bed, with no shirt on. It reminds me of when I would watch him in the shower. Will he touch himself when he's watching me? Liquid trickles into my underwear at the thought.

When Lincoln is done, he comes to the side of the bed and pulls my hair back until it stings, and I'm meeting his eye. "I asked, do you understand?" There's a glimmer of excitement in his eyes, but also a hardness. A thrill of fear runs through me. He's as exciting as he is frightening. He slaps me lightly across the face - it's more shocking than painful, and I gasp.

"Yes... yes, sir," I stammer.

He keeps his hold on my hair and pulls it to the side, bringing tears to my eyes. With his other hand, he pinches a nipple - hard. I cry out and squirm against my bonds.

Indignation rises in me, and Irene's senses perk up. But she senses more sexual excitement than fear, and she falls dormant again. She knows I want this, even if my conscious self is unsure. And she wants me to fix things with the boys.

More wetness spills into my underwear as he speaks into my ear. "Tell me why you need to be punished, Cassia?"

"I... I... lied to you. And I ran away. I used Irene to tie you up, sir."

"You put yourself in danger," he says, and I hear the anger in his words now. He moves to my other nipple, and I arch and gasp at the fresh pain.

The pain suddenly releases, and I find Lincoln's mouth on mine. He kisses me like I'm the air he needs to breathe, and his need makes me whimper. When he's done, I'm left panting. He presses his forehead to mine and puts a hand on my throat. "You made us worry."

Then he pulls back, grabs my hair and pinches my nipple hard again. "Now Brad thinks you want to leave. Do you want to leave, Cassia?"

"No! No, I don't want to leave, sir."

"Why did you lie then, Cassia? Why did you run away?" His voice ends on a questing note, his gaze searching mine. He's genuinely asking.

But the words won't come. When I hesitate to answer, his finger on my nipple squeezes harder. Tears leak out of my eyes as I squeeze them shut and shudder at the pain. I cry out, but he ignores me. I'm spread open here, exposed to both of them, and for a moment it really does feel like torture. He's asking me to tell him things I've barely admitted to myself.

"Answer me," he says. His voice is commanding, but casual. He's not barking an order at me, he's confident that I'll respond, sooner or later. It's a patient voice. No matter what I do, no matter how much I fight it, Lincoln won't let me go.

It's strangely comforting. I open my eyes again and meet his gaze directly. Surprise flickers in his eyes.

"You won't stop until I answer, will you?" I whisper. I don't mean the words to come out like a plea. And I forget to say sir. He doesn't seem to mind.

"No, Cassia. I won't stop." It should be a threat, but it comes out like a promise.

"You belong with us," Brad says, from the screen. Lincoln doesn't say it, but an approving half-smile plays on his lips.

"Answer the question," Lincoln says, and tightens his grip on my hair, lifting my head back and placing a hand on my throat. "Brad deserves an answer."

"Because I was scared," I whisper. He stills at that, and a stony mask falls over his face. Despite our positions, I realise how much power I hold over this man. And how much I just hurt him, without meaning to.

He eases his grip on my hair, and something in me wails with loss. I'm not ready for tonight to be over. "Wait, Lincoln..." He's still looking at me, but I can feel his retreat. I wish my hands were free to reach for him.

But the only way I can get him back is with words. Desperately, I reach for Irene, and hear her speak through my body.

*"She's not scared of you, Lincoln. She's scared to trust. Men have left her. She knows I'll never leave her. Humans are so complicated."*

"Fuck," Brad says, through the phone. "She's still completely entwined with Irene."

"Interesting," Lincoln says. "We seem to have you back. You know your eyes went green just then?"

I shake my head, and he wraps his hand around my hair painfully, jerking my head back. My eyes squeeze shut. "Well, you cheated, and you forgot to say sir. But if that was the only way you could get the truth out... you've been a good girl," he says.

He strokes a finger between my legs, causing me to gasp for other reasons. My thighs clench, but I can't move them closer together. My panties are soaking. He makes a satisfied sound in his throat when he feels me.

Abruptly, his hands leave me. When my eyes open, he's looking at me again, gaze considering as he strokes my face. "You never have to worry about us leaving, Cassia. Brad's right, you belong with us." The frankness in his voice leaves me blinking. I know Lincoln isn't a simple man, and I think he's been through as much turmoil as I have in the past couple of months. I wasn't expecting this blunt declaration. He says it like he believes it - like it's the truth.

It leaves me feeling more exposed than my spread-eagled position, but gladly so, given this glimpse behind the curtain at this complex man.

"Now for your punishment." A smile plays on his lips - a rare thing, and my stomach swoops as he brings a metal implement to my face - it's a metal rod with a spiked wheel that rotates on the end. It looks nasty.

I glance up at the phone where Brad is watching. His eyes are heavy-lidded with lust. I look back at Lincoln. He's not touching me right now, and my body is melting with anticipation.

I lick my lips. "Yes, sir."

# Chapter Ten

# LINCOLN

C assia's confession was moving, but she still isn't telling me everything. She's not as good a liar as she thinks. The fact she could rip Irene from our control tonight was disturbing. But it's hard to focus on that right now.

I run the spiked wheel along Cassia's stomach, watching her every reaction as the sharp metal bites into her flesh. Her gaze is fixed on me, and it's intoxicating.

Her skin is goose-pimpled, and she makes little gasps when I press harder. I run the wheel along her cleavage, and across the erect nubs of her nipples, where they sit taut against the fabric of her barely there bra. It leaves little red marks, but I'm careful not to pierce the skin. She whimpers and squirms as I press harder.

Her pleasure - that's what's causing my pants to tent. That's something people misunderstand about what I do in the bedroom. Women approach me with a measure of fear and excitement, but everything I do serves them. I fulfill fantasies, and I take pride in it.

I only engage with a woman when I can feel she wants to be punished so deeply it's like a need. That's what I felt from Cass when she took off her jacket. That delicious mingling of fear and arousal. Her submission.

I know this is going to be complicated. But it was impossible to say no. She needed it - I felt it in her confession. And I needed it too, after she's avoided me all this time.

I push aside the fabric of her bra and squeeze a nipple, running the sharp edge of the wheel hard against her skin. She cries out, and the smell of her arousal fills my nostrils - strawberries and musk, with a salty edge. She reacts well to pain. Better than I'd hoped.

I enjoy how her eyelids flutter closed, but I want her attention more. "Look at me," I command.

"Yes, sir," she says breathlessly. Her voice is submissive, but her gaze is anything but. Cassia is always a challenge - she's always fighting.

And she's been on her own for a long time. I suppose it was natural for her to keep things from us - she had to keep things from the coven for years. It still hurts that she lied.

Tonight, she won't be able to - pleasure and pain are too simple for lies.

"I expect your eyes to always be on me, Cassia," I say. "Now I'm going to ensure Brad has a better view." I fight my impatience and let the vines take their time unraveling and pulling her soaking panties off. I'm careful not to touch her, to alleviate her lust.

She makes a soft sound of surprise as the vines part her legs and spread her splayed wide, her wet sex and round ass fully visible to the camera. She's on her back with her legs over her head, totally exposed. "That's more appropriate for our bratty girl. How's that, brother?"

"Looks good," he says, his voice rough with desire. I'm glad he's here for this - I wouldn't feel comfortable doing this without him.

"Now I'm going to punish you, Cassia, and it's going to hurt. Only when you've taken your punishment like a good girl, will you get your reward."

I notice with satisfaction when she clocks my erection and swallows. I'm hard as a rock, and it's a challenge to move so slowly, but the anticipation is worth the wait.

I stand to the side of the bed when I land my first blow to her right buttock. I hit hard. She gasps and twitches. The last time I did this, Brad was helping, and we both went easier. I land blows, alternating softer and harder, so she's not sure what she's going to get next.

"Are you sorry for what you did, Cassia?"

"Yes, sir," she gasps, squirming. She's breathless.

When she's nice and red, I walk around the bed and work the other cheek. Her eyes track me.

"Will you do it again, Cassia?"

"No, sir," she says. She shuffles on the bed as if to squirm away from me, but I'm not fooled. She's afraid of the pain, but she's dripping wet. I keep landing blows, alternating cheeks.

"Tell me you're sorry, Cassia,"

"I'm sorry sir, I'm so sorry." Her mascara is running now, smarting from tears streaming down her face. I stop spanking her. Her ass is glowing red, but her gaze is still fixed on mine.

I walk to her head and mount the bed, coming up beside her to reach over and dip my hand to her pussy, spreading her lips to show Brad how wet she is. Her whole body shudders, and I can't help myself. I lean over and find her lips. I kiss her sweetly, letting her set the pace. Soon she's whimpering against me, pushing against her bonds, and fresh wetness spills over my hand where I'm still holding her open.

I won't last long. But after her confession tonight, I can't just take her. This isn't just about me. "Brother, I think you'd better get down here."

# Chapter Eleven

# CASSIA

It takes fifteen minutes for Brad to arrive. In that time, Lincoln doesn't touch my sex again. Instead, he kisses me and lets his vines tighten around me, compressing my body further, squeezing around my limbs.

It's painful, but it intensifies the need pulsing through my core.

In this strange position, he puts gentle kisses on my mouth, on my cheeks, and nibbles at my ears, while he calls me a good girl for taking my punishment.

When Brad arrives, I'm groaning with need. My face heats when Lincoln lets him in. Brad's wearing a motorcycle jacket, a t-shirt and black jeans. His eyes are wide, almost feverish, as he approaches the bed.

He runs a light hand along my ass, reminding me of the blows Lincoln landed on me earlier. I squirm against my bonds, hoping he'll touch my sex.

"I think we should keep our witch waiting," Lincoln says gently, and I groan in frustration.

Brad grins at him in acknowledgement. "Brought something," he suggests, and holds up a vial of pink love potion. It's my new, modified recipe. Guaranteed not to work on plants.

Lincoln raises an eyebrow. "What do you think, Cassia? Is this safe in your condition?"

I hesitate. The potion is safe to use with the boys, but they still don't know the full extent of my powers. And I suspect that's because Irene doesn't want them to know. She stirs uneasily, and I can feel her compelling me to say no.

But I'm done lying. It's not the time to explain everything, but I want the boys to know. I want them to feel everything about me.

Brad's gaze draws hungrily to my sex, and he says, "You can rub it into skin?"

I push Irene aside and say, "Yes."

She pouts, and I declare a silent victory.

Brad squirts some of the potion into his mouth, and hands it to Lincoln, who does the same.

Then Brad strips - quickly and easily, down to nothing, his erection springing free. My breath catches when he approaches the foot of the bed and puts some potion in his hands before putting the vial on the bed beside me. He rubs it into my sore ass-cheeks. Now and then, his fingers stray close to my sex.

Beside me, Lincoln is also undressing. He moves slowly, taking off his cravat first, and throwing each piece of clothing onto a nearby couch. He's leaner than Brad, but fit and more hard-bodied than I'd guessed. I suppose he always had to support Brad in the endless fights he told me he got into when they were young. His cock is surprising, too - bigger than I would have expected from his frame.

Lincoln approaches my head and Brad hands Lincoln the vial. Lincoln pours a liberal amount on my breasts, rubbing it in. To reach my breasts, he has to mount the bed, and navigate between my feet that are still thrown over my head. His impressive erection bobs near my head. Lincoln has a fresher scent than Brad's musky cedarwood. Lincoln smells more like pinewood, and right now it smells delicious.

Soon my body is tingling all over, and I'm getting wafts of lust from the boys. The only sounds in the room are our breathing.

I know they can feel me too when their hands slow down, and Lincoln pinches and tugs at my nipples in sync with the rhythm of my pleasure. Brad's fingers knead harder at my ass, fingers brushing against the sensitive skin around my anus.

I'm whimpering helplessly when Lincoln finally lowers his cock to my mouth. It's salty with pre-cum, and I take it in hungrily as he holds the back of my hair. "Good girl," he says. "Take it all in." I take him in further than I've ever taken a man before, and feel him in the back of my throat, driven by the feedback of his pleasure, and the toying of Brad's fingers at my anus.

When Brad finally presses his erection into my soaking sex, I'm more than ready. "This is what you need, isn't it?" he says, as he slides his silky length into me.

My eyes roll back in my head with pleasure. Lincoln's fingers tighten in my hair and he presses himself even further into my throat as they both take me in a consistent rhythm.

I feel consumed by them - utterly taken, my body singing with pleasure. I'm on the edge of an explosive climax when Lincoln pulls out of my mouth and says, "my turn."

The boys both step back and the vines flip me disorientingly fast. I'm on my hands and knees, and my hands are bound underneath me, propping me up precariously with my face towards the couch. Lincoln is behind me on the bed, Brad is in front, and has stood back.

The vines twist and turn around me, and I soon feel thin stripes of pain, like the pinwheel toy Lincoln was using earlier. I look down to find thorns in the vines, twisting around my body and striping white marks as they scrape along my skin.

If I strain against them, they'll pierce my skin. Around my thighs, more thorns scrape, and I yelp in surprise as one pierces my skin right near my sex. The surprising zing of pain goes straight to my core and I gasp.

"The thorns will hurt. This is a punishment," Lincoln says from behind me.

Brad is turning the couch in front of me around, and flops down on it, his erection pointing towards me. He's enjoying the show. I look at him with wide eyes as a vine wraps around my neck and mouth.

"Don't look at me like that," Brad smiles, his gaze never leaving my face. "Your body loves it."

He's right - the pain, the discomfort, the humiliation - my body feels like it's on fire. And being the center of attention of both gorgeous boys doesn't hurt either.

Leaves curl around me next and flutter around my clitoris. My eyes roll back and I groan against my gag. Thorny vines wrap around my nipples and squeeze, and I squeal. I'm not sure I can take any more. And that's before the insistent pressure of a finger in my anus.

My eyes fly open, and I look at Brad again. His cock is in his hand now, and his eyes are heavy lidded. "Take it like a good girl," he says, as Lincoln's finger breaches me.

I can't move because of the thorns that restrain me, so I shut my eyes and feel every inch of his finger inside me, and the vines that twist more insistently at my nipples. The leaves around my clitoris stroke me gently in a consistent rhythm. When the orgasm starts, it's like a quaking coming from deep within me, fed by the waves of pleasure coming off both the boys.

When I think I can't handle any more, Brad steps forward and the vines unwrap from my mouth. I make a nonsensical sound of need when I take him into my mouth.

# Chapter Twelve

# BRAD

It's a good thing we're not very conventional, my brother and I. When Lincoln says it's his turn, I knew they would both enjoy their time together, but I didn't realize how much it would turn me on watching him toy with her.

I'm glad I brought the mind meld, too. I knew it was a risk, since Cassia's initial connection with Irene was caused by mind meld potion, but I feel the need for the closeness with her tonight. And I need to know she's enjoying herself under Lincoln's administrations.

I wish I could see her from every angle, but I can feel every pulse of pleasure that quivers through her body. Lincoln pushes her further than I ever would. I let him lead. I've had Cassia for two months now, and this is his first chance. And I'm taking notes. Lincoln is a master of torturing women with pleasure. He's kneeling behind her on the bed, face pressed in concentration, keeping her on the edge of release.

She holds her breath - I can feel it - as he toys with her. I love that her eyes are fixed on me, trusting me to ground her. Her trust, her love, flows through the connection between us.

I don't need her to tell me that she's taking this step for us, for me. I already knew Lincoln was the missing piece.

Her eyes go dark with lust as I press my cock into her wet, open mouth.

Behind her, Lincoln pulls the finger from her ass and slowly breaches her pussy with his cock. I'm not a small guy, so I'm comfortable saying that Lincoln is big. But I know my girl can handle it.

He doesn't go easy on her. Her body's more than ready. It's singing - on fire. He takes her hard, gripping at the vines at her waist to pummel into her. We've shared women before, but I've never seen him take someone with this punishing intensity.

She loves every second. She's no longer humiliated - she's straining hard against her bonds, pushing into the thorns that wrap around her.

Every piercing thorn is an explosion of pain that elevates her pleasure. I feel it all as her mouth smacks back and forward along my cock, plunging me deep down her mouth. Her whole body is shaking, and she's whimpering against my cock, tears leaking out of the corners of her eyes.

Her body is overflowing with pleasure, and she's a slave to it, her constant hunger finally satiated. It's like she's where she truly belongs. Lincoln creeps a finger back into her anus, and her whole body shudders as her release grips her.

It comes on with the devastation of a Richter scale earthquake. I'm immersed in her, and it feels like my soul is ripped from my body, for a moment soaring entirely free, broken by a wave of intensity that shatters all thought into a million pieces. It's a purity I've never experienced.

There's no way either Lincoln nor I can resist drowning in her wave. He releases into her with a guttural curse that sounds entirely unlike him, and I come deep down her throat, while she sucks on me hungrily, even through her pleasure.

Cassia's orgasms are like coming home, and she's never come like this before.

The vines around Cassia withdraw so she can collapse, exhausted, onto the bed. I crawl into bed beside her and pull her to me.

There are little pin pricks all over her body. But she's smiling, and happy, when she kisses me. She always loves sex, but right now, she's more at peace than I've seen her for a long time. Lincoln gets up and grabs the healing cream for her wounds.

When I pull back, I put a hand to her face, and a wave of emotion comes off her. Peace, happiness, love. It's like a tsunami heading straight for me, and I can't help the words that come out of my mouth. "I love you."

For a moment she looks shocked, and I hold my breath. Then a beaming smile breaks out across her face. "I love you too," she says, and kisses me.

From the edge of the bed, I feel Lincoln's hesitation. He's not unhappy, exactly, but he's unsure where he fits.

I want to tell him he's included in this, that he's a part of it, that he made it happen. But I feel something nagging at the corner of my thoughts. Something we had blocked out, with our intense focus on pleasure.

Cassia frowns and I can feel rather than hear Irene, embedded deeply within Cassia's consciousness, sounding an alarm. There's something wrong at the house.

Cassia's thoughts run underground, connecting with the roots of the trees in the surrounding buildings, right back to Irene, in our back garden.

I exchange a look with Lincoln. We could do that, with effort, but until a few weeks ago, I would have said no witch could.

A muscle twitches in Lincoln's cheek. He's genuinely angry now, and in this state, I wouldn't let him near Cassia with a whip for both their sakes. "How long has she been able to do that?" he asks.

# Chapter Thirteen
## CASSIA

We ride back to the house in Lincoln's Mercedes in silence, Brad ahead of us on the motorbike.

On the way there, I call Olivia. "Something's happening at the boys' house," I say. I don't bother saying hello. I'm only getting impressions from Irene, but I can feel orcs are involved.

Olivia doesn't wait for more information. "On our way there." She doesn't qualify who she's bringing with her.

When I hang up the phone, I'm left in the stony silence, with only the air-conditioning making a sound. Guilt eats at my stomach.

Even without the alarm from Irene, I'd be overwhelmed by tonight. It was a lot to take in - both of the brothers working together. I saw the expression on Lincoln's face, felt it in his caresses. He cares about me. And Brad loves me. My chest hurts when I think of his confession, and if

I weren't so torn up inside right now, I'd be singing. He loves me even though I kept things from him.

Maybe I'm messed up, but when I was growing up, I didn't have a proper family. Nobody ever cared enough about me to punish me. I was on my own. I got into my own scrapes, and I got myself out of them. The only thing I was praised for was my magic, and nobody saw how hard I worked on my spells - they only saw the results.

I'm not used to being loved.

Tonight showed me they care about me, and they care if I put myself in danger. They'll fight for me, and it's more than I deserve.

I can't help but think of Michael and wonder who loves him. His parents were as indifferent to him growing up as my foster families were to me. His card is still in my pocket. He said all he wants to do is talk. Don't I owe that to an old friend?

Irene is not convinced Michael is worth it, despite having access to my memories. She might be more mine than the boys now, but she's still loyal to them.

"I knew you'd find out, I just didn't have time to explain," I say out loud. I wish I was wearing something more than damp lingerie and a trench coat right now. I also wish Brad was here. But maybe it's okay that he's not - Lincoln and I have had little time to ourselves. Tonight was the start of something, and now I might have broken my relationship with both boys.

"What else have you been hiding?" he asks.

It's understandable he doesn't trust me. So I tell him. I tell him about my blackouts and how tired I've been. I tell him the blackouts are the reason for my broken arm. He watches the road intently and says nothing.

Because he's silent, I babble. I tell him everything I told Brad about Michael - that he was my only friend and made life at the coven bearable. That I don't want him like that. "It feels like he has an answer to whatever's happening with Irene and me," I say. Lincoln doesn't answer, eyes steady on the road in front of him.

In the back of my mind, Irene stirs restlessly. She's no longer connected to the brothers, but she doesn't like when Lincoln is upset. Her misery adds to my own.

When we reach the house, Brad's motorbike is in the driveway, along with Olivia's nondescript Toyota. Irene carpets the front lawn, reaching for me when I arrive.

This close, I get impressions more clearly from her. "An orc tried to break in. Olivia stopped him, but he got away," I say, as she winds herself around my ankles. She doesn't slow me down as I walk swiftly with Lincoln through the front door.

When we see who's inside, Lincoln's jaw tenses.

In the kitchen, Tom Johnson, billionaire and orc shifter, is sitting at the kitchen table, drinking tea. He's in human form, but he's still an imposing figure. His presence fills the room.

His beautiful fiancé and half orc Mystic, Summer, is sitting beside him. She smiles at me and I can't help but smile back. This is the woman who had a vision that I could help them prevent a war.

Olivia is on the other side of her. She nods at me. Brad is standing - it looks like he just beat us here. He looks over at me and Lincoln, as if trying to assess the mood. The love potion has faded, and I wish I knew what he was thinking. He told me he loved me and then found out I'd been lying to him. Again.

"Do you know who tried to break in?" I ask Olivia.

"Of course they do," Lincoln says. He's standing, arms folded, looking warily at Tom. He was much like this when he first met Olivia, too. Mages don't trust orcs - and Lincoln doesn't trust anyone.

Brad pulls up a chair beside Olivia and rocks it back on its hind legs. Lincoln leans back against a kitchen counter. I stay standing.

"I wish I came with better news," Tom starts. "But my people are on the brink of war. I believe it was my brother, Evan, who came here tonight. He's also been working with the Fairbridge coven. He's old fashioned and believes that orcs shouldn't try to assimilate into the human world. He had some followers before I found Summer."

Summer takes over smoothly and puts a hand over Tom's where he holds his tea cup. I've never seen a power couple in real life before. "Once Evan knew mystics existed, we weren't sure what he was going to do."

"Or what other orcs would do," Olivia says.

Tom continues. "Fortunately, many of the orcs joined my people. I have a facility where they're safe." He glances at Summer here. "It was pure luck I found Summer, and we don't know if there are more mystics out there, but that's what's keeping the people loyal to me. The belief that we can find more mystics. But not everyone believes we can. Some of our people still believe in Evan, and he's looking for something that makes him as desirable a leader as I am right now."

"But Evan has found another solution," Summer says.

"The Fairbridge coven magic that allows orcs to impregnate witches," Lincoln says.

"Yes," says Summer. "The only problem is, we've found some women who've been impregnated. And although the orcs can indeed have sex under the spell, that doesn't mean the women can bear orcish children. Some of the injuries that have been reported of women who've had sex with orcs are because of the incompatibilities of genital size. But some of those are women who have been actually impregnated. We couldn't figure out how until we heard about the witches spelling the orcs."

"Human women aren't equipped to breed orc babies," Olivia says, shaking her head. "The fetuses need more energy, which apparently hurts. A lot."

"So, what can we do?" I ask.

Here Summer and Tom exchange an uneasy look. "We don't know, to be honest. Olivia thinks of you as the tangled witch, and since it's your coven, that's the one dealing with the orcs - that's too much of a coincidence for us to ignore. We decided it was time to finally meet you and see what you thought of all this. Maybe we can come up with a solution together."

My stomach churns as they all stare at me. Lincoln was right. The last time he was teasing me about my orcish connections. They think I'm special, but they don't know how.

"What do the witches get out of dealing with the orcs?" Lincoln asks.

"We think they're using orc blood in their spells," Olivia says.

I look at her sharply. The churning in my stomach intensifies.

"A witch named Michael Thompson seems to be pushing the charge. He's been calling for the use of the orc blood and leading the negotiations," Tom says.

Lincoln and Brad both stare at me, and my blood roars in my ears. I only hear snippets of the next part of the conversation - Lincoln and Brad saying they met him.

Memories rise to the surface of my mind, to when a teenage Michael seemed obsessed with any way to amplify his meagre power.

"Cassia was friends with him," Lincoln says, turning to me. His lips are pressed into a thin line.

"That true, Cass?" Olivia asks. Concern crinkles her eyes.

I shake my head. "Michael was... my first friend. He was my only friend in the coven."

"And was he a good person?" she asks. They all look at me.

"Well..." I think back. "He was who I think he had to be, given he had limited powers. Attention seeking, sometimes demanding, sometimes dramatic. He would have temper tantrums like a spoiled child, well after he was old enough to do so. He could be frightening, throwing things, red-faced. But then later, laughing, shrugging off 'crazy Michael.'"

"How did he seem when you saw him at the coven?" Olivia asks.

I shake my head again, trying to wipe the memories. "He's different. He's more confident now. I can see that people follow him. But I wish I'd had the chance to talk to him. It's only then I'd know for sure."

"He's dangerous, Cass," she says firmly.

She might be right. But I also remember that Michael was my friend. And he was teased and overlooked compared to our peers who mastered magic well, and desperate for acceptance and attention. Just like me. And look how great I turned out. Can I really judge?

"Is there anything that would make you think he would turn out like this?" she asks.

I shake my head.

"Do you know what impact orc blood would have on a witch's spells?" Summer asks. "We've only heard rumors, but it would be great to understand more about it."

I shake my head numbly. I've never heard of blood being used in magic before.

"What about Mrs. Maisley? She's the only other witch we know, right?" Brad suggests.

"She never answers the door to us," Lincoln says.

"She might answer the door to another witch?" Brad says, and looks at me, where I'm still trying to find my breath.

———— ≈ ————

I'm glad to walk outside, into the cool night air, away from the eyes watching me, towards Mrs. Maisley's front door. I've changed into a more respectable dress. My stomach is still roiling, taking in all the information from tonight.

Her house is run down - not as well done up as the boys', or now, mine. She answers the door, peeking her head out.

"I was wondering when you'd pop by. What with orcs crawling all over your property," she says. She has a soft Scottish accent, but her eyes are sharp as she looks at me.

I assumed she was from an international coven, and never asked why she left. She's always seemed like a sweet old lady who wants to be left alone. I wanted the same thing when we first met, so I respected her wishes. Then she says, "And you with those two mages. Your mother would roll over in her grave, young lady."

It's my turn to give her a sharp look. "You knew my mother?"

She opens the door, ushering me in, and looks around to see if anyone is coming after me. "It's time you came in."

Over a cup of tea, we sit in Mrs. Maisley's charming cottage. The run-down exterior hides a charming old house, full of quaint furniture and rustic touches.

"Your mother was a firecracker, just like you. She came to see me when she left the coven. I told her, if she needed me, she could always come back and find me. Lost witches find each other, did you know?"

I shake my head mutely. I didn't know that, but I had known that Mrs. Maisley was a witch from the charms she hung out around her house.

"Were you from a coven in Scotland?"

"Aye."

"And they're okay with people leaving in your coven?"

"They don't love it, but sometimes they understand it's for the best. And they don't mind when it's someone with no special talents. Not like your mother - I knew her magic from the moment I saw her. I sense it in you too - a glow about you. You're something special. I knew they wouldn't let her be and told her as much. I have a few connections with local witches, and heard they never found her. Good for her."

She sniffs disdainfully. "Your coven isn't very smart. All they could see in you and your mother was a way to make money."

"And have you heard of Michael Thompson?"

"Hah! I'm not surprised he's involved. A savvy politician, that one, and your coven has been weak. Your mother's spells were the only thing propping them up. They were desperate after you left - and with the protection from your mages, keeping you safe, they've had few options."

"I've heard Michael wants to use orc blood in spells. Is that possible?"

"Aye. Spells use energy from blood, the way many covens use sex, but sex is natural, and sits well with magic. Blood is more powerful, but addictive."

I'm bewildered. "Why haven't I heard of it?"

"Because it's banned in most covens. With good reason."

She's answering with riddles. But I only have more questions. "What would orc blood do?" I ask.

She shakes her head. "Nothing good," she says. She turns sharply to the door, and she gets up and walks to the window. "But I expect we'll all see the results of it soon. But right now, you have company."

I look out the window with her.

Two black cars stop outside my door. Four orcs and four male witches roll out and head for my house.

# Chapter Fourteen

## BRAD

Lincoln's staring out the window at Cassia's house. Neither of us like Cassia being away from us right now. Hearing how dangerous Michael is... I'm not sure why he let us go, but I have no doubt it's part of a bigger game.

It's strange to think how short a time we've known each other. Before this, she belonged to the witch's world, and we belong to the mages. Since we've been together, it hasn't seemed to matter. And now she's changing. Her powers are almost mage-like now.

Irene's connection screams through us, and Lincoln and I exchange a look. I rush to join him at the window.

"What is it?" Olivia asks. I guess there's no orc special sense about trouble. Olivia, Tom and Summer join us at the window.

Four orcs and four men - witches, from their simple black garb - are approaching Cassia's house. They don't bother knocking. An orc kicks the door down instead, and they pour inside.

Lincoln curses beside me. Cassia admitted her wards weren't very good. It was on the list of things we were meaning to do - get a ward witch from an unrelated coven out. But with everything that has been going on, and Cassia's business taking off, we hadn't gotten around to it.

After the events two months ago, we didn't think we'd have any need.

Lincoln heads for our front door. I follow, hands already curling into fists, and behind me, I feel a ripple in reality as the orcs transform.

When we get outside, Tom roars, chillingly loud. Olivia joins him, and Summer hisses - her skin has colored purple, unlike Olivia and Tom's green, but she looks just as vicious. Her limbs have grown long and sleek. It's a primal challenge - and the orcs who've invaded Cassia's house respond.

All four of the orcs come out of Cassia's house, leaving the witches inside.

Lincoln enters first, ducking a spell thrown at him that melts the wall beside him.

There are house plants throughout Cassia's house, and I sense as he activates each of them - tripping up the first two witches in the house and attempting to bind the second.

It won't be enough, but the waving vines slow them down. Two of them turn back to tackle us, and the other two keep going - looking for Cassia, while plants uproot themselves to stop them.

Irene could push through the windows, break the walls - break the floor - but Cassia just fixed this house. Besides, I don't think we have to do that yet.

I grin as one of the witches comes at me with his fists. He gets in a punch to the face before I headbutt him, hearing his nose crunch. Lincoln is engaged with another witch while the two behind him try to untangle themselves. I forget what it's like to watch him fight - he's precise, face frowning in concentration, and fast on his feet. Lincoln rarely gets hit in fistfights, unlike me. He ducks a blow and punches the man in the gut - hard. He's hit in just the right spot that the man curls over, retching.

And then Tom is in the doorway behind us, walking past to take on the two witches escaping the vines Lincoln trussed them in. He knocks the two out easily by banging their heads together. They collapse onto the floor.

The fight is over, and Cassia's house is almost unscathed.

Out on the lawn, Olivia and Summer are still standing, and the four orcs who attacked them are already in one of the vehicles, driving off. I exchange a look with Olivia.

"We know who they are," she says. "We'll take care of them later."

Lincoln says it first. "Where's Cassia?"

Dread creeps into my stomach. She's nowhere to be seen, but I pull my phone out of my pocket and see a message waiting for me.

> I won't run. I'm going to talk to Michael – Cassia

# Chapter Fifteen

## CASSIA

I head to the door, but Mrs. Maisley's hand on my arm stops me. "I have to help," I say.

She speaks urgently. "You have to run and hide." She shakes her head. "Maybe if it was just your old coven, you'd have a chance. But Michael has united at least two. And now orcs are involved. Eventually they'll find you. And you won't always be surrounded by your orc friends."

I look out the window again at my beautiful house. Lincoln and Brad are running outside now, and the orcs are roaring as they enter the fight. Tom pummels one orc hard in the nose and knocks him out almost immediately. The thud from the force of the blow shocks me.

She's right - Brad wouldn't be able to take a blow from an orc like that without dying. And he wouldn't be in this situation if it wasn't for me. The boys keep fighting for me, and if Mrs. Maisley is right, they could be fighting for a long time. This isn't just about me - they deserve a life, too.

Tonight was incredible. It felt right. If I were a better person, I'd leave. I'd leave them both and give them a chance at a happier life. But I guess I'm not that good a person. I can't willingly walk away from either of them.

It's taken me so long to find a home that's mine, and it might be destroyed tonight. Again. By the same people who ruined it last time.

"Why do they want me so badly?" I ask. It's a plaintive wail, driven by the urgent need to protect Lincoln and Brad. Irene stirs inside me, ready to fight. But Mrs. Maisley's hand is like a vise on my arm.

She shakes her head, frustrated. "I don't know. But they're not what they seem, child - nobody had even heard of your coven until a few generations ago. It's like they just appeared out of nowhere. They're dangerous. And they won't stop coming for you."

She's right again. I watch as Tom, Olivia and Summer take down the three orcs on the lawn. Olivia's people have resources - they could keep us safe. But that means giving up the life I've worked so hard to build.

What's happening out on the lawn isn't the actual fight. I need to know what the coven wants from me.

I don't want to leave the boys. That's not my intention. But I have to know - I have to know about Michael. He has the answers. He's the last thread.

I take my phone out of my pocket and dial Michael's number. After we talk, I text Brad.

# CHAPTER SIXTEEN

## CASSIA

It's strange to be in the same hotel room the boys and I shared only hours ago. The bed is neatly made, and I can't smell sex in the air, thankfully. The key was easy to get - we'd returned it earlier, and the front desk people had seen me leaving.

I wouldn't make the mistake of going back to the coven, but I also couldn't talk to Michael in a public place. He'd agreed to bring my mother's grimoire pages, and we could talk. We could strike a deal.

And I feel strong here, surrounded by lush plants. They seem to whisper to me, feeling my tension and soothing it. I close my eyes, feeling the vines crawling up the walls outside the building.

When there's a knock at the door, my heart leaps in my chest, but I think I'm ready.

I take a deep breath and open the door.

The angry orc with the missing hand wraps a thick fist around my neck and lifts me off the ground. My feet kick helplessly as he steps me inside. I can't take my eyes off him - his eyes are red, and he looks mean. He's huge - as large as Tom looked from where I watched him in my front garden.

Behind him, Michael closes the door behind him, and barks, "Put her down! That is completely unnecessary."

The orc scowls in my face. "All this fuss over a little girl." Black dots dance in front of my eyes, but he drops me before I pass out. I fall to the floor and start coughing immediately.

Inside me, Irene seethes, but I tell her to back down. Not yet. I need answers.

"If you can't act civilized, you can wait outside, just in case her friends come for her," Michael says. He glares at the orc.

From my position on the ground, I look between them. Michael doesn't look afraid, but the orc is much bigger than him.

Still, it's the orc who backs down and steps outside the room, leaving me alone with Michael.

"I'm sorry about him," he says. "I wouldn't deal with the orcs if it wasn't necessary." He's wearing plain black clothing - simple and cotton, like the coven prefers. And he's holding a black satchel. He offers me a hand up, and when I'm standing, he pulls a handful of old pages out of his bag. "A peace offering. That's what you're here for, right? Your mother's missing grimoire pages?"

I take them from him warily. "Thank you," I say, still rubbing my neck. I flick through the pages. They're all there.

"They're a lie, of course," he says, as he makes his way to the minibar. It's tucked into the hallway leading into the open-plan hotel room. He takes out a miniature bottle of scotch. He shakes it at me as if offering it to me, but I ignore him. He's different - brusque, and not warm like he was last time I saw him. He doesn't remind me so much of our old friendship now.

"What do you mean, a lie?"

He shrugs and grabs a glass, pouring the scotch into it. "Oh, the grimoire was your mother's, and the spells are real, but the ageing of the pages isn't. The browning, all of that - it's magically been made to look older." He takes a sip of scotch and looks at the bottle with his nose wrinkled.

"Why would they do that?" I ask. The handwriting on the pages is consistent with my mother's grimoire.

"The coven does it with everything. They surround themselves in antiques, they age their grimoires, they emulate the old ways. But the coven is new - only four generations old. And they're not really a coven, of course," he says. He leans back against the kitchenette in the small hotel room.

I stare at him blankly.

"They weren't a coven four generations ago. They were one of the other kinds of magic user. My guess is shifters. But they lost their magic. Sometimes it happens, you know - there's no explanation for it. Something in the water, something in the food, chemicals, global warming - for whatever reason, their magic was drying up. They covered it for as long as they could, but then one of them realized that they had enough magic in them to do witchcraft. So that's what they did. There is no coven. It's all made up - even that three-headed snake sigil they use. It means nothing." He shrugs, his head shaking, as if in acceptance of something he's known for a long time.

It's information that floors me. But I believe him - Michael was always researching obsessively about the history of our magic. If anyone would have uncovered a secret like this, it's him. "How do you know all this?" I ask.

"Everyone knew, at some point. But people forgot. I dug it up when I was researching how to make magic stronger. It was all there, in the old, dusty books that nobody bothers reading anymore. The really old ones." He rolls the scotch around in its glass.

"How do I fit into this?" I ask.

"Well, your mother was a powerful witch. And those binding spells of hers - they're stronger than anything most covens can muster. Possibly because she specialized in binding spells, and shifters are basically magically bound to another creature." He sips his scotch, but barely looks at me, inspecting his glass. Something feels off. He's edgy, distracted. His hand is shaking around the glass.

"She knew something was different about her magic. But the coven could only see dollar signs. They didn't want her experimenting. So she ran away to the mages. Without those pages you're holding, her grimoire wouldn't work for her. When I heard you'd formed a mind meld with a plant... well, I had to see you for myself." He turns to look at me for the first time. His eyes are as intent on me as they were the other day, but it's not desire in them. It's a different kind of greed.

I take a step back, towards the door. It's involuntary, and I know the orc is outside. I've made a terrible mistake and I'm not sure how to get out of it. "So now you've seen me. What does the coven want?"

"The coven? Hah! They want you back because they're broke, and they can't handle the competition from your business. They always had limited imaginations." He steps forward, a manic gleam in his eye. "You're more than that. You can make us all stronger."

I fold my arms around myself and look away from him, shaking my head in denial and shuffling my feet back further, mind whirling. There are plants in this room. A lot of them. I begin connecting with each of them, feeling them agree to my will. "I'm not... I'm nothing special," I say out loud.

"But you are," he says, and reaches for his satchel, rummaging inside. "You could be the key. Rejoin the coven, join the council, have a place by my side. Marry me."

"What?" I ask, alarmed, looking at him with shock. Whatever hold I had on the plants in the room breaks suddenly. He smiles and pulls a box out of his satchel. He opens the box - it's a small, diamond ring.

My heart stops. Have I misread the situation? But his expression isn't loving. It's cynical. He's making me an offer like a business deal, one eyebrow cocked at me in question. And his eyes - they're sharp, predatory, and not with lust. I shake my head, backing away and waving my hands. "No, Michael. I don't want this."

He closes the box with a click and throws it on the bed, then picks up his glass again, walking towards me with a shrug.

"Well, it was worth a shot. I guess those mages are keeping you too busy," he says. "Although lord knows how long it'll last until they tire of you." His cruel words sting. The idea that he might remember some of the friendship of our childhood now seems laughable.

"I'm leaving now. Don't come after me again," I say, raising my hands. The plants around us stir and grow quickly, spreading towards him.

"I was afraid you'd say that. But it's okay, I don't need you to come with me. I just need a little blood."

He throws his drink at me, and the pungent smell of a sleeping potion fills the room.

# Chapter Seventeen

# LINCOLN

B rad reads me the message Cassia sent us and starts heading towards his bike.

Me? I'm angry. She left us - again. She's put herself in danger again. Whatever submission Cassia pretends to have is only that - she's a danger to herself, and right now, she's a danger to my brother.

I can't help wonder how much this evening's activities added to her desire to see Michael again. Was it too much? Was I too much? Pleasure in the moment is one thing - but I don't know how Cassia feels about me now. And in the time she should be processing, she's run away to meet a man we know means her harm.

I'm not as convinced as Brad is that she wants to be with him romantically, but I am convinced he'll try to lure her away from us.

"Stop," I call out to him. "Where are you going?"

He turns around but is still walking backwards. "To go find her," he says. He turns around and keeps walking.

"Where do you think she is?" I ask. He stops, turns around and looks at me. "She wouldn't go back to the coven. She's not that stupid."

Olivia joins me. "He's right," she says. Around us, Summer and Tom are trussing up the witches. "Is there anywhere else she might go? Somewhere neutral?"

Brad shakes his head. "If we get it wrong, we could miss her."

"I know who knows where she is," I say. I walk towards our house. Brad follows me as I head to the backyard. I kneel in the dirt, putting my hands on Irene's vines, right near the root of her. "Irene, we only want to protect her."

A wave of stubbornness comes through the vine, but it feels distant. I can't believe it's taken me this long to realize how much Irene has pulled away from us.

"Irene, please," Brad says, joining me. "I love her. She loves me. Don't you want us to be together?"

Another wave of stubbornness, and a vague impression of Brad and Cassia arguing. "But we fixed all that, Irene," I say. "We fixed all that tonight." Flashbacks of our night in the hotel room come back to me.

"We just want to be together, Irene," Brad says.

"All of us," I say, quietly. I focus on an image of Cassia, in the hotel room from earlier tonight... but fully clothed.

And it clicks. "I have the hotel room for the rest of the night," I say. "It's a neutral place. She's meeting him there."

Brad exchanges a look with me.

"One more stop first," I say. "Let's find out what the old witch said to her."

\*\*\*

When we're in the car, Brad is quiet, wheels turning in his head, processing what the witch told us. After we talked to her, we both grabbed knives, just in case. With multiple covens after her, we don't know what to expect.

I say it out loud for both of us. "Her magic isn't like anything I've felt before. She's more than a witch. It's like she's fully merged with Irene."

I don't expect Brad to answer. After a pause, he says, "When Irene and Cassia were first bound, and she was unconscious, she came to me in the night. She wasn't herself. It felt more like Irene. I think she was acting instinctively, seeking sexual energy to heal. It kind of freaked me out."

"And in the morning, she was fine," I say, remembering the day.

"Maybe her blackouts are a kind of transition," Brad adds.

He's smarter than I give him credit for, sometimes. Puberty is when a mage's full power comes in, and we spend a lot of time sleeping. "Her body is changing and adjusting," I agree.

"But she wasn't tired today," he says, with a frown.

I exchange a look with him. "Maybe she's done adjusting."

He shakes his head. "Whatever. She belongs with us, whatever she shifts into."

As he says this, we pull up at the hotel. I stop the car in a parking bay outside and turn off the engine. "Let's hope her shifted self wants us too," I say.

# CHAPTER EIGHTEEN

# BRAD

I guess we thought we'd be rescuing her. But then that's what we thought we were doing last night too, and she didn't need much rescuing then either.

When we knock on the hotel room door, there isn't an answer. Lincoln taps me and gestures with his eyes to the floor, where I see leaves peeking out from under the door. That's when I know it's unlikely Cassia is going to be a damsel in distress tonight.

There isn't an answer, but when I turn the door handle, it's unlocked. Lincoln and I exchange a look and I swing the door open.

There's a wall of shrubbery blocking our way. We both put our hands on it and will the shrubs to move. They don't. I push harder, but they don't budge.

I reach for the knives tucked into each boot. Lincoln has a knife out and ready, but he puts a hand on my arm. "Let's try persuasion," he says.

He sends gentle suggestions this time, images of the lights in the hallway. Being plants, they naturally grow towards the light anyway.... I join his persuasive push, and the shrubbery spreads along the walls into the hallway, making a gap for us to walk through. I pull my knives out now.

Inside, we see a giant orc with one hand trussed up against one wall. He struggles and makes muffled roars. As we watch, one giant orc fist punches out of the mass of vines covering him, but they swarm, pinning him back. On the other wall, Michael is almost entirely engulfed in vines.

Cassia is sitting on the edge of the bed, vines crawling over every part of her, eyes open and entirely dark green. Vines grow out of her fingertips, joining the flow of vines around her. They're what's keeping the orc and Michael contained.

The ones by the door are the rest of the plants that were in the room. I suspect that's the only reason we could move them.

The only corner of the room not covered in vines is the glass window, letting light from a bright streetlight stream in for the plants.

As we walk into the room, I notice all the taps in the bathroom are running on full blast. Inside the bathroom, vines cover every surface, and are hungrily gathered around the sink, bath and shower taps.

We ignore them as we walk slowly up to Cassia.

"Hello, pretty witch," Lincoln says, and I've got to give him credit - he sounds calm and not completely freaked out like I am.

Cassia doesn't respond. She continues staring straight ahead, lost somewhere inside herself.

Frustration rises inside me, and I walk up to Michael on the wall and move the vines away from his face. He gasps when his mouth is free. I do it carefully. The vines have huge thorns in them, the full size of my finger. One has pierced his right cheek. I don't dare cut them - I'm not sure how Cassia will react.

Now I'm up close, I can see the red dripping on the vines around him, and onto a mass of vines at his feet. He's bleeding hard.

"What happened?" I ask him.

"I just wanted a bit of her blood. I used a sleeping potion, but she... she turned into..." He stares at her in horror, but there's a glint of something greedy in his eyes. "She's shifted." He says it with a whisper.

I resist the urge to punch him in the face. Yes, he's trussed up and helpless, but the guy pisses me off. "What do you know about it?"

He splutters out something about Cassia's people descending from shifters. I bark a laugh. I had heard shifters were real, but I've never met one. And I'd never heard of a shifter who merges with plants before. "So she's a were-plant?" I ask.

He looks at me with wide frightened eyes, and I leave him where he is, letting the vines slowly wrap once again around his mouth. I'm not sure I could stop them if I tried.

Lincoln is still standing in front of Cassia's blank face, trying to get her attention with her name, or Irene's. "If she's a shifter, then she's still in there."

"He said he used a sleeping potion on her. She might be fighting it off."

"She's definitely feeding," Lincoln agrees. He shoots a look back at me. "But is she feeding her plant, or her magic? Plants like blood and bone, but the old woman said using blood wasn't a good idea. Especially orc blood. That might be why she's in this state."

At that moment, the orc rips his arm free of the vines, and uses it to free his other arm. Thick thorns stab him, and vines come out to hold him down. He chews through the vines at his mouth and roars.

"Let's help him," Lincoln says. "We want him away from her. And we're not getting through to her like this."

When my first knife cuts through the vines around the orc, Cassia turns her mouth to us and screams. It's a chilling, inhuman sound. Vines unwind from the wall, whipping towards us. One makes a deep cut along my cheek.

The vines abruptly stop, waving still in the air, and Cassia blinks. A look of confusion comes over her face. "Brad?" she asks. It doesn't sound like her, but it's the voice I remember, from the night she came to my room when it seemed as if she was possessed.

The orc rips free of the wall and lumbers to the glass window, throwing himself out of it onto the street one level below. We don't bother looking after him.

The noise, and the sudden rush of fresh air, seem to agitate Irene. Cassia's face hardens again. The vines waving in the air grab Lincoln and me and throw us against the wall. My knives clatter to the ground.

# Chapter Nineteen

# LINCOLN

I brace myself, expecting the worst, when the vines wrap around me, but somehow the sharp thorns never pierce my skin, and my face is free. And I've held on to my knife. Irene doesn't seem to care.

"It's good to have you here, my boys," she purrs.

Across the wall from us both, Michael's face is covered in vines completely now. I want him to die, but I don't think Cassia would want that. "We're here, Irene. Why don't you let Michael go? You don't need him," I say.

"He tried to hurt us. I need to heal."

I remember this is Irene I'm dealing with, not Cassia. Irene, my pet, my long-time companion. Sullen, childish Irene, who sometimes needs discipline. "You seemed healed well enough, Irene," I say sharply. "Why don't you let the witch go? His blood isn't good for you."

She pouts, her dark eyes sullen. "But he tastes good," she says.

"Too much will make you sick," I say sternly.

"You're so mean, Lincoln," she says, frowning, like a child having a tantrum.

"Lincoln's right, Irene. It's not good for you. Let him go and we can take you home and back to the garden you love. Wouldn't you like that?" Brad says.

She turns towards him, distracted, and I see my chance. Vines fall off her so there's only a trail at her feet, and the vines flowing from her hands. Her face fills with glee. "I don't have roots anymore, Brad! I can go anywhere I want. You could come with me!" He always spoiled her.

"Mostly I just want to go home," he says. His eyes are fixed on her, and pointedly not looking at me.

"I bet I could convince you to come with me," she says, and vines rip at her dress, shredding it around her. "You like Cassia's body, don't you?" I'm temporarily distracted from severing the surrounding vines as Irene strips Cassia's body. Fortunately, she's distracted enough not to notice my cuts. When she's fully naked, she presses closer to Brad.

I pull out of the bonds at my arm, cut my other arm free, and swing with my knife. My legs are still attached to the wall, so I throw my whole body weight down hard against her right arm and the vines growing from it.

My swing severs through the vines there completely, and she screams. Brad drops from the wall, and half the vines around Michael unravel, revealing his unconscious, unmoving body. He looks dead.

I only have a moment to look at Brad before Irene has me slammed back up against the wall, vines swarming. The thorns aren't so gentle this time, but they only make shallow cuts. Cassia's right hand is back to normal. She ignores Brad completely as her vines swarm him from her left arm.

Brad steps in front of her and kisses her, one hand on her lower back, the other on her cheek.

For a moment she's stiff. But I see her body soften against his. There's desperation in his action, like he's trying to funnel all his need into that kiss.

"I will follow you anywhere," he says, when he pulls up for air. The love in that statement strikes deep in my chest. If there's anything that could bring her back, it's Brad's love for her.

For a moment, it seems to have worked. Her eyes are brown again. Her expression is slack. But she blinks back to green, and a mischievous light fills her eyes as she smiles. "I think you both need to be punished first. That's what you like, isn't it?" Vines wrap around Brad again and he's pinned to the wall next to me, and his clothes are ripped from his body.

Michael's body is on the opposite wall, and blood still drips beneath him, feeding writhing vines.

"It's polite to finish eating before sex," I say, looking pointedly at Michael.

To my relief, she pouts, and vines extend to carry his body out the window, dropping it inelegantly to the ground floor below. A distant crash announces it falling to the ground.

That's all the blood taken care of. This gives me some hope that she'll return to normal. And she doesn't seem interested in feeding on my blood, or Brad's. Yet.

Thorns press closer and vines tug harder at me, and my clothing is torn and shredded off me too.

The pull and tight sense of binding of the vines, and the sight of Cassia naked before me, looking at me in triumph, sends a wave of desire through my body. By the time I'm fully naked, my erection is unmistakable.

Irene saunters up to me, and her vines painfully push me higher up the wall so my cock is even with her mouth. "This is how Cassia does it, isn't it?" she says, and works my cock with her fist.

I grit my teeth. Vines creep up to wrap around my neck, stomach and biceps. Thorns scrape along my arms, drawing thin red lines. I'm determined not to groan, but the bindings at my neck tighten, and my vision blacks at the edges.

"Easy, Irene," Brad says.

"Cassia, I know you're in there," I say. "Don't let her do this to me." It comes out in gasps.

"Huh," she says. "He can give punishment but can't take it. And you need to be punished, Lincoln. The witches and orcs knew way more about Cassia than they should have. Vera's the only person who could have told them. You've been very, very bad."

Her revelation sends a shockwave of sick guilt to my gut. I thought I'd been so careful with Vera. But I knew she couldn't be trusted. And how many little things did I mention? How many opportunities did she have to go through my things when I wasn't in the room? I should have known.

"You deserve your punishment, Lincoln," Irene says, and I relax as much as I can in my bonds. She's right. If Vera has anything to do with Cassia being in this much trouble, I do deserve to be punished.

Something releases in my chest at that thought. I've always been the one doling out punishment, and I've seen the release in my submissive's face when they submit to me. Now I understand that feeling. There's nothing I can do in this situation but take whatever Irene wants to give me.

Maybe after that she'll let Cassia come back. Cassia won't be gone forever, hopefully. And there has to be some of her in there, driving this. Irene might be violent and bloodthirsty, twisted by drinking blood, but Cassia told me she's not interested in sex. By contrast, Cassia is always hungry for more.

"Please punish me, Cassia," I squeeze out, hoping she can hear me. I can't see her eyes enough to know if it works, with my head forced back, but I feel a wet finger probing at my anus. When she breaches me, I squeeze my eyes shut. When she works my shaft as well, I groan deeply.

I won't last long this way.

"Please punish me, mistress," I plead mindlessly. There's no response but her fist pumping my shaft. Surely Irene would be bored by now if it were just her?

When she sneaks another finger into my ass, my back arches, but I'm restrained by the vines. My whole body trembles when the vines around my waist tighten, pressing the thorns into me with exquisite points of pain. When a sharp thorn pierces my right nipple, I come with an uncontrollable shout.

"Lincoln?" she asks. I'm dizzy in the aftermath of my orgasm and can only feel the vines lowering me to the ground. When my feet hit the ground, Cassia's hand is on my face, her soft brown eyes on mine. "Are you okay?"

It takes me a moment to realize it's her. She's back to herself. I put a hand over where hers is resting on my face and kiss her more deeply than I ever have before. It's the most delicious thing I've ever tasted.

When she pulls back, her eyes are dark with desire, but she licks her lips as if shaking it off.

"I'm so sorry," she says. She looks back at Brad and I can see he's been freed too and sporting a rock hard erection. He joins us, holding her from behind. It feels right, having her pressed between us. "I could feel everything happening, but I couldn't stop it. I've got Irene reined in now."

"Well, at least we know what brings you back to yourself," Brad murmurs, kissing her neck. "Lincoln's cum."

She coughs a laugh, which turns into a gasp as I stroke a finger along her wet pussy as evidence. "He's partly right. Sexual energy seems to bring you back into your body. But we might need to be sure you've got things under control."

I kiss her again, and put my arms around her neck, before raising an eyebrow at Brad. I hold her in place while he enters her from behind.

"For the record," I say into her ear as I toy with her clitoris and she moans between us. "I'd follow you anywhere, too."

# Chapter Twenty

# CASSIA

I'm in the garden two weeks later. Not the boys' garden - mine. It's a fresh spring day. What was once a tangled patch of weeds is now a thriving witch's garden, herbs growing in neat, obedient rows, and a lemon, red apple and lime tree behind them. A vine extends from my hand and I pick a fresh apple from the tree.

I can feel it all now - every living plant around me. The bees pollinating the flowers, the wind through my leaves. My senses have expanded, and are not only limited to this garden. Deep underground. It's like I have my own roots - roots of magic, stretching far beyond my skin. The sense of limitlessness has extended into my spellcrafting. I'm no longer worried that I haven't mastered my mother's spells yet. I know it will happen.

My grimoire knitted itself back together as soon as the missing pages touched the frayed edges they were ripped from, and the spells feel more complete somehow when I weave them.

Irene is here with me, but the boys and I have had plenty of time to experiment, and we have her tamed, but I also haven't been under the level of stress I was two weeks ago. The coven backed off after Michael's death. Without his leadership, there's nothing to unite the covens, which Mrs. Maisley says means I'm safe, for now.

It was hard to process that Irene killed Michael, and we've had long conversations about morality. Fortunately, she was deeply affected by drinking orc blood, and is horrified at his murder. I'm in a more harmonious place with my shifter self.

"I see you're getting used to that," Lincoln says, coming up behind me.

I take a bite, letting the vines that have replaced my hands hold it for me.

"Want one?" I say, around a mouthful. He shakes his head. I can tell from the tense line of his shoulders something is wrong.

"You worry too much, Lincoln," Irene says through my mouth. "How could you think so much when you have all these exciting senses?" He quirks a smile at her and she hands him the half-eaten apple. The boys know when she's talking because my eyes change color, apparently. He takes the apple this time and has a bite. He sucks on his lower lip as some juice squeezes down. Then he winks at me.

I catch my breath and return to my body as he hands me back the apple.

Lincoln's become an expert at knowing what turns me on, and that instantly pushes Irene out of my body. He smiles knowingly at me.

My eyes only tear away from him as Brad jogs out of the house, shirtless, in shorts. He's just been for a run and he's sweaty all over. His shoulders glisten with a new tan in the sunshine. He leans in for a light kiss. He tastes salty, and he playfully licks at my lips before stealing the apple, and retreating and standing back next to his brother.

"I suppose that will work too," Lincoln says wryly, watching me ogle his brother.

"Did you tell her?" Brad asks, a bit breathless from his run. "Tom's brother Evan has emerged again," Brad says. "And he's kidnapped Summer's sister."

His words still my libido. The first prophecy Summer had was that divided blood would flow. That's what I think happened in the hotel room. The second prophecy was that the tangled witch would help them. After finding out I'm really a shifter, all tangled up with a plant, I'm not even sure if that still applies to me.

But I remember Evan - the twisted, dark look on his face when I saw him in the hotel room. He's full of rage. I feel for Summer's sister, and I'll help if I can.

Lincoln continues. "Olivia tracked them down, but there's some situation with them being trapped in a cave, deep underground, and it's a fragile area - we're worried if we try to get in, they'll get a cave in. But there are root systems in those parts. Do you think you could help?"

I nod. It's what I've been waiting for. All the doubt I've been carrying about my place with the orcs is rising to the surface. But instead of keeping it inside, I say it out loud this time. "I hope I can help."

Lincoln comes up and puts a hand on my face. It still catches my breath, this new intimacy between us. "We'll help. You're not alone."

Behind him, Brad nods. "And if Irene gets out of hand, well..." He smiles. "That could be fun, too." Inside me, Irene rolls her eyes.

***

## What next?

Want to find out what Olivia's been up to? Find out in <u>Mated to the Sapphic Orc</u>

# FREE BOOK

Claim your free copy of Taming the office orc. It's about a shy witch who can't do magic, a charismatic orc making his own way in the human world, and the sparks that fly when they meet.

You can claim the story, and find out more about me at
**authorlamonteiro.com**
Or @AuthorLAMonteiro on Instagram, TikTok and Facebook.

# THANKS TO...

The Katharine Susannah Prichard Writers' Centre. This book was completed during a two week fellowship in a writers' cabin in Perth, Australia.

Laura Goldstraw, Avis Kokal, Melony Phillips and Elisabeth Copeland for beta reading – ie helping impose order on chaos.

# MORE BY THE AUTHOR

**The Zodiac Monster Romance Series**

Taken by Aries

Taken by Taurus

Taken by Gemini

---

**The Seasonal Spice Series**

Taming the Office Orc (Prequel)

50 Shades of Orc

Bound by the Mages

The Witch's Tangle

Mated to the Sapphic Orc

Kidnapped by the Orc

Claimed by the Orc

## Springvale Book Club

Hot for the Bad Boys

Hot for the Mafia Men

---

## Standalones

The Wild Side

---

## Anthologies

Lights

Batteries

Silk

www.ingramcontent.com/pod-product-compliance
Lightning Source LLC
Chambersburg PA
CBHW070544120726
47909CB00007B/2231